UNLUCKY CHARM

Second Edition

Aidan Lucid

First published in January 2022

Re-published in October 2024

Published by Aidan Lucid.

Book Design by: Aidan Lucid

Front cover illustration by Smstudioinc
(https://www.fiverr.com/smstudioinc)

Back cover by Get Covers

For more information about Aidan Lucid or his books, go to:
www.aidanlucidauthor.com

ACKNOWLEDGMENTS

I'd like to thank the following:

Beta readers: D_Pamela, Simonadarkthrill and Manusrichangal from Fiverr for their excellent input.

Editors: Lisa at Hidden Gems, D_Pamela and Olivia K. Logan for your fantastic work

Smstudioinc for producing yet another fantastic cover.

My good friend, Dawn Schware, for the medical advice in the ambulance scene.

God for giving me the gift of writing.

And finally, you, for purchasing this novella.

Thanks and God bless you all.

BOOKS BY THIS AUTHOR

The Zargothian Saga Series

The Lost Son (Second Edition)
Deadly Pursuits
When Worlds Collide (2026)
Jasper's Christmas Adventure (winter 2026)

Hopps Town Series

The Scavenger (Second Edition)
Unlucky Charm (Second Edition)
Dark Secrets
Lurking Beasts (fall 2025)

Short Fiction

A Beast Within
The Perfect Christmas Gift (Short story)

PRAISE FOR, *THE SCAVENGER*

"The Scavenger is a nail-biting story with lots of nail-biting excitement. It was hard to put down. 4.5 fun spooky stars!"

- Priscilla Bettis, author.

"A coming-of-age story with heavy allegorical elements, the themes Lucid explores are important and timely. Blending fantastical elements with relatable relationships, authentic dialogue, and common struggles too often left undiscussed, this book does what YA literature should always strive for – educate, entertain, and inspire."

- Self-Publishing Review

"Lots of people have played with the 'magical wish gone wrong' idea, but Lucid did it with more finesse and subtlety than most writers."

Gilbert Stack, owner of, The Imaginary Realms of Gilbert Stack Blog

“There's a creeping paranormal here amongst the normal, that tingles those hairs on the back of your neck."

- Geoff Nelder, award-winning author of, Aria trilogy.

PART ONE: THE GIFT

A smile of satisfaction spread across Jared's face as he relished the cool softness of his pillow. It was good to be back home from college for two weeks. He had missed being here, the smell of freshly washed bed clothes and his mom's home-cooked meals.

The last year had been a rollercoaster of emotions. Jared never expected to encounter a demon and ghost after making a wish in the cursed well with Jessica and Adrian. He still had nightmares about the exorcism he did at the well with Aunt Maybelle to get rid of the demon and Caleb Hammerson's ghost. Although it happened twelve months ago, the sinister chill he felt at that place never left him.

In the months that followed and with Maybelle's guidance, he honed his powers by meditating and praying. Some spirits came to him and he helped them cross over. There were still sometimes the boy would nearly jump out of his chair or bed when a dead person would walk through the dormitory walls to ask for help. This took some getting used to but Jared coped by continually practicing the meditations Maybelle gave him.

Drifting off to sleep, the sound of humming coming from the hallway roused him from his slumber.

"Ma, knock it off," he mumbled before turning over on his side.

Just as he was about to close his eyes, a sweet soft humming came from the hallway once more.

"Dammit Ma," Jared grumbled, swinging both legs from underneath the duvet, stomping out of his room.

Looking in both directions, Jared couldn't see anyone. His parents' bedroom door was closed.

Maybe I was dreaming the whole thing. He was about to return to bed when in his peripheral vision, he saw the end of a frilly dress entering the kitchen. It was like the ones seen in the old cowboy movies his dad, Oscar, loved to watch.

He followed the female spirit into the kitchen.

There, standing with her back to him was a tall, black lady dressed in a light blue, elegant 19th-century plaid dress. Her hair was tied up in a large bun. A gold ring was on her left index finger.

"Ex— excuse me, miss," Jared stuttered, "are you okay?"

While floating in mid-air she pivoted to face him. Her brown pupils were stressed by the whites of her eyes. The ghost brimmed with an aura of authority. Jared could sense that this woman had power when she was alive. A witch possibly, he surmised.

"Those brigands took what don't belong to them." She spoke with what Jared thought was a French accent, her voice filled with hurt and urgency.

"Who took what from you?"

"They know not the perils."

"Wait a second. Hold up. What are you talking about, ma'am?"

Staring down at her feet she took a deep breath, trying to remain patient. Her eyes were filled with pleading as she looked back at him again. "Monsieur, find it or it shall be too late."

The kitchen light's luminance increased to an almost blinding level. Jared shielded his face with both hands for a few seconds until the light had returned to normal. Once his eyes were re-adjusted, he could see that the woman had disappeared.

"Where'd she go?" he asked himself while giving a quick glance around. Popping his head out the door, Jared surveyed the hallway but it was empty.

What is it I gotta find? Sure seemed important to her.

Returning to bed, Jared tried many times to sleep. Her warning kept reverberating around his mind. He couldn't shake the feeling that someone was in a lot of trouble. The question was who, and what could he do to help them?

***

Zane Miller, a 24-year-old six-footer with a ginger crew cut, in a beige store uniform, locked the doors to "Jamie's" - a family-owned mom-and-pop store. He had just finished his eight-hour shift. Zane rubbed his hands together while blowing on them. Frost lingered in the air and he whistled while walking to his Renault Clio, glad to be going home.

Just as Zane was nearing the car, an old lady passed him, her face caked in dirt. An acrid stench wafted from her. She dragged a bulging suitcase behind her. The lady rummaged through some pockets in a long, tattered, camel-colored trench coat. A ten-dollar bill fell out of the pocket but the woman walked on unaware. Zane waited a few seconds to see if she'd notice. It remained on the ground as the vagrant walked on further.

"Well, thank you, ma'am," he said while picking up the wrinkled note.

Suddenly, shouts could be heard coming from the opposite side of the car park. Two men in their twenties, who had NFL footballer physiques and were wearing white tracksuit bottoms and sweaters, were pushing and shoving a lanky kid in his mid-teens. One man slapped him, knocking off his glasses. The teen had a bag full of groceries ripped from his hand, canned food and fresh vegetables spilling everywhere.

"Good luck with that, kid," Zane said while getting into the car. Gunning the engine, sounds of heavy metal music belted out through his speakers. Switching on the headlights, he pulled out of his parking space and stopped at the entrance to Jamie's car park, waiting for traffic to pass. In his rear-view mirror, Zane could see both men pushing the teenager to the ground, kicking the groceries as if they were footballs.

Memories of being bullied in high school came flooding back. Many times Zane would wander home, trying to hide bruised ribs when jocks would punch him, stealing what little lunch money he had. A pang of sympathy for the kid hit him.

"Damn," he cursed, hitting the steering wheel. Signaling right, he did a U-turn, parking close to where the fight was. Popping the trunk, Zane took out a baseball bat.

"Hey guys," Zane cried out, walking closer.

Both men stopped as he wielded the bat, swinging it about.

"This is none of your business," one man replied. "Get lost."

"I'm making it my business. Why don't you try pushing me around, huh?" Now he gripped the weapon, ready to knock off one or both of their heads.

Taking one look at the boy still on the ground, both bullies backed away, wandering up the street.

Zane lent his hand, helping the kid get up.

"Thanks," he said in a meek voice, brushing dirt off of his red t-shirt and black shorts.

From his trunk, Zane took out a spare plastic bag. He picked up the canned food items, putting them into it. "You got a name?"

"Billy," the boy said, fixing his scruffy blond hair.

He gave the bag to Billy. "How did the fight start?"

"They made fun of my t-shirt and I told them to go screw themselves. That's when they started pushing me."

"Take it from someone who knows, sometimes it's best to say nothing and walk on."

"I think I'll do that in future."

Zane watched Billy put on his glasses.

"You live far from here?"

"No, just a few minutes' walk." Billy took what remained of the bag of groceries, leaving the now dirty produce behind. He looked unsure what to do next.

"I'll get the rest of this," Zane assured him. "Go home, your parents might be worried about you."

"Thanks mister," Billy replied, avoiding eye contact, his head lowered and shoulders slouched while walking away.

Zane knew how Billy felt. Once or twice someone came to his rescue but he was so overcome with shame for not being able to stand up for himself that he didn't know how to thank the rescuer.

Picking up the vegetables, he threw them into the nearest trash can and went home.

***

Zane closed the door of his two-bedroom apartment and sank into the couch, putting his legs up on the small, mahogany coffee table. Only the four avocado-green walls with a mixture of family pictures and photos of his Little League playing days kept him company. Sometimes Zane wished he had a woman to cuddle up with at night to watch some TV or go for walks with at the weekends. He never had much luck with girls, feeling awkward and jittery around them, never knowing what to say. In Zane's mind, his father was to blame for that, always calling him a 'pansy' for never having a girlfriend.

Taking a bottle of beer from the fridge, a date circled in black on a sports calendar caught his attention. Zane cursed when he saw this. It was his father's birthday soon. Even though he still had some hatred toward the man, his mother would be angry if he didn't get him a present.

Tomorrow after work, I'll order something online. The usual go-to New York Nicks t-shirt or boxing's greatest fights DVD would keep Dick happy. Last year Margery scolded Zane for not making more of an effort, but he refrained from telling her that 'dear old dad' was lucky to be getting anything at all. His parents were copy editors at a large publishing house.

The sounds of wrestlers slamming each other filled the living room when he switched on the TV, causing all thoughts of birthday gifts to be cast aside.

***

Reggie Danes and his girlfriend, Monica Walker, flopped breathlessly onto their bed. Reggie smoothed down his long, dirty brown hair. His forehead glistened with beads of sweat.

"Was that good for you?" Monica asked, pulling bedclothes around her toned, naked body.

"Sure was. You?"

"Did you not hear me moan?" She lay her head on his chest.

"Yeah, think the whole neighborhood did." She laughed as he said this. He loved the smell of the new coconut-scented shampoo coming from her auburn hair.

Reggie felt fortunate that Monica, who was beautiful with model-like features, wanted to be with him. He'd caught Zane secretly watching her a few times.

Reggie had met Monica nine months ago at the garage where he worked. Her carburettor had been faulty and one tire had blown out, so she had to get it towed. From the moment they met, there was a 'spark' between them. He liked her sense of humor and she his, even some of the crude jokes. The woman caused him to raise his eyebrows more than once when she swore often.

He had moved into her house two weeks ago, and their relationship blossomed even more as they got to know and understand one another better.

One thing that Reggie didn't like was their bedroom. Monica insisted on keeping her tulip pink wallpaper. If that didn't already make him feel emasculated, there were fluffy orange photo frames on the dressing table. In them were pictures of her family and friends. Many times Reggie felt the urge to throw out the frames or pretend he accidentally broke them, but he refrained from doing so to avoid hurting Monica.

"You know, I was thinking," Reggie said, choosing his words carefully, as he tried to pluck up some courage. "Maybe we could change the room a little."

"Really? You want to talk about that now after what we just did?"

"Why not?"

"Okay," she replied, her tone a combination of surprise and slight annoyance. "What's wrong with it?"

"Can we make it less...girly?"

"How?"

"Change the wallpaper or paint the walls a different color."

There was silence at first as Monica mulled over her answer. After what seemed like a few minutes, she replied, "I like this wallpaper. It's been here for a while."

"Yeah, but I'm here now. Can we give it a more…neutral color?"

"Yeah, sure. I'm open to change."

That went well. Reggie sighed with relief while getting out of bed. "Gotta take a whiz."

"Need a hand?" Monica joked.

"I'm good. Got two of my own," Reggie said with a wink while waving both palms.

***

Zane sat in the car, eyeing a bunch of his DVDs and video games sitting next to him on the front passenger seat. He hated parting with them, but there were too many lying around. He needed the extra space and cash.

Giving one last sigh of regret, Zane picked up the bundle and went into Mr. Stevenson's Pawn Shop.

When he opened the door, a ding from a bell greeted him. This place had been a video game arcade until five years ago. There were many fond memories of him and Reggie spending hours, and nearly all their weekly pocket money here. He remembered slotting quarters into the machines, sometimes in the elusive hope of winning a cuddly toy. Then Ron Stevenson bought the place, turning it into the only pawn store in Hopps Town. They adorned the walls with expensive TVs, game consoles, rare collectibles, and other valuable items. Zane just thought of it all as junk folks wanted to buy.

Ron's hulking frame stepped out from the plastic drapes separating the backroom from the store. Looking at him, one would think that he belonged to a biker gang with his long white beard and leather jacket that couldn't fit around his pot belly. A navy bandana with an American eagle was on his head.

"Hello there," Ron boomed in his deep, husky voice. "What can I do for you?"

"How much can I get for these?" Zane asked, holding up the bundle.

"Let me take a look." Ron opened each case, inspecting the discs. When finished, he stared at them for a moment, sizing up their worth. "How about forty bucks?"

"Can you do better than that?"

Smacking his lips, Ron studied the items for another few seconds. "I can stretch to fifty, but no more."

Zane ran a hand through his crew cut, feeling like someone punched him in the gut. Fifty Dollars for all this, especially some games that were only a few months old, seemed like a low-ball figure. Then again, he thought it was better than going home empty-handed.

"Okay, I'll take it."

"My man," Ron said with a smile while shaking Zane's hand. "I'll just take these to the storeroom and will give you the cash in a minute." Gathering up the bundle, Ron stepped through the drapes.

While Zane waited for his money, he stared at the jewelry section in front of him. There, glistening under the light, was a shiny silver pocket watch. Unusual engravings like those of some unknown alphabet curled around a symbol of a square. Two diagonal lines were on either side of it. The watch seemed to call to him, making Zane want it even more.

Maybe mom might like this. His mother loved antiques. The watch would be a perfect Mother's Day gift.

Ron returned with a clipboard and five ten-dollar bills, laying them out on the glass counter. "Here you go, sir. I just need you to fill out your details here." He handed over the clipboard.

"How much for that pocket watch?" Zane asked while writing his address.

"That's new. Just came in yesterday."

"Okay, but how much?"

"One hundred and ninety bucks. Why? You want it?"

"Yeah," Zane answered, hoping for a large discount.

"Tell you what, since I've seen you here a few times before, I'll give it to you for one twenty."

Score, Zane thought. Yes, it meant he'd be coming out with no cash, but he really wanted it for his mother. "All right." He gave Ron a fifty and a twenty-dollar bill on top of what was on the counter.

Ron put the money in the cash register before writing up a receipt. Taking out the pocket watch, he slid it into a small paper bag.

"Whoever that's intended for, hope they like it."

"Yeah, me too." Zane stuffed the bag into his coat and left.

***

Zane gave a customer he'd just rung up his change and said goodbye. The man nodded his head in gratitude and left. Zane's eyes lit up and he smiled upon seeing Reggie stepping up to the counter, holding a can of soda and a candy bar.

"Hey, Z. How are you, man?"

"I'm good, bro'. You on a quick break?"
"Yeah, just here to get these."
"That's four bucks."
Reggie shot Zane a stunned look. "Are you serious? Four bucks for those?" he asked while raising both items.
"I know but hey, it's Robertson who sets the prices."
"That's extortion."
"Tell me about it."
Reggie reluctantly reached into his pocket and pulled out a five-dollar bill.
"Thanks." Zane took a dollar change from the register, handing it back to his friend. Looking left and right, he reached under the cash register to pull out a small bag. "I got something to show you." He opened the paper bag and took out the silver pocket watch.
"Whoa, nice piece of jewelry there, bud."
"It's for my mom. Got it in Stevenson's Pawn Shop this morning."
"Can I hold it?"
"Sure. Here." Zane dropped it into Reggie's hand.
"Feels a little heavy," he said, lifting his hand up and down with the beautiful object in the center of his palm. "Must be worth a pretty penny despite the funny markings on it."
"Stevenson gave me a discount. Just hope Mom likes it."
"I'm sure she will." Reggie put the watch back into Zane's hand again. "I gotta bounce. Catch ya later, Z."
"See you." Zane put his mother's gift into the bag again, wrapping it up before he placed it underneath the cash register.

***

Turning the key in the lock, Reggie opened the door and entered his apartment.

Sitting down on the couch, he pressed a button on the remote control to switch on the TV. Excited commentary greeted him as an NFL player scored a touchdown. A few hours before, Monica had texted to let him know she'd be late. Her boss was working on a case and he needed extra notes typed up for court, which meant she'd have to work overtime.

Sleep had eluded him lately, waking up three or four nights a week around 3 am. Then he remembered the first aid cabinet in the kitchen. Monica always kept some sleeping medication in there. A few months ago, she suffered two weeks of insomnia. Even though he hated taking medicine of any kind, Reggie guessed it might help him get some sleep.

Putting what remained of his beer into the refrigerator, Reggie popped a pill from its packaging into his palm. With a glass of water he swallowed it, waiting for the tiredness to take over.

After thirty more minutes of watching the match, his eyes became too heavy to keep open. Soon his head dropped, and this was a sign that it was time to go to bed.

Later, caught in the midst of a pleasant dream, Reggie smiled, dreaming that he was lying on a sun-drenched beach. Suddenly, he heard a scream and saw a girl with a stomach wound standing on the shore.

Reggie sat straight up panting. He recognized the girl from a past event that was too traumatic to ever forget.

"It's all right. It's over now," Reggie reminded himself. *But why did she come to me now, after all this time?*

He laid down again. It took him a few minutes to drift off.

Later, and with a wide grin, Reggie felt Monica's fingers running through his hair. This always calmed him and brought back memories of when they first started dating. Every Sunday, they'd sit under a large tree in the park, his head on her lap. He'd look up at the sunshine filtering through leafy branches while her fingers combed through his hair.

"That's nice, hon," Reggie muttered, his words a little slurred while still half-dreaming.

The sound of their front door being closed woke him completely, along with Monica calling out his name. "Reg, are you up?"

Frozen stiff with fear, Reggie stared straight ahead and didn't answer. *Who the hell was stroking my hair just now?*

"Hey, baby, are you—" Monica stopped when she saw him lying in bed. Reggie closed both eyes, pretending to be asleep. She shut the door and went to the kitchen. He opened his eyes again, taking deep breaths, trying not to panic.

Did I imagine that? Was it even real? One thing was for certain: there would not be much sleep tonight either.

***

Zane sank into his couch, his legs aching from standing all day. Taking off both shoes, he massaged his ankles. Propping an orange pillow behind him, he laid his head on it. Zane flicked through the channels stopping when a sitcom he loved came on.

Suddenly, his eyebrows rose in surprise when the TV switched off.

"What the…?" he asked himself while pressing the power button on the remote. The screen came alive again with a commercial about a new superhero series airing on that channel.

"Weird," Zane muttered.

A few seconds had passed when the screen went blank again.

"What the hell?" he muttered, pressing the power button again. The superhero commercial just finished when the set came back on. *Weird.*

He froze while entering the kitchen. Every cupboard door creaked open simultaneously by themselves.

"Holy…crap!" Zane muttered; his eyes widened in horror.

Music blared from his cell phone, snapping him out of his shock. It was a tune that triggered a horrifying childhood memory. "Dream a Little Dream of Me" made him break out in a cold sweat. He retreated a few steps, his heart hammering against his chest.

"What's going on here?" he said, snatching up the phone and ending the YouTube video. Grabbing his car keys, he ran out of the apartment.

Parked on top of Bunker Hill, Zane stared out at the town's lights. Couples usually reserved this place for their more intimate moments, but he didn't care about that right now. He was still trying to figure out what had just happened. Did a ghost suddenly come into his home? Did he really want to be there?

Ghosts and the paranormal were something his family never believed in. When he was a kid, the Miller household didn't observe Halloween. His father, Donald Miller, scared away trick-or-treaters when he'd answer the door holding his replica sawn-off shotgun. Kids always ran screaming in terror. Zane chuckled the first time Donald did it, but after a while, nobody would play with him at school, except for Reggie. Any time an episode of, *A Haunting,* came on, he laughed at the poltergeist activity and spooky happenings the victims went through. Now it wasn't funny anymore. A part of him was afraid to go back.

Heck, I can't stay here all night, Zane thought. Turning the dial, he put on the radio for an hour, listening to old country music songs until it was time to go home.

***

Jared sat watching TV in the living room. His parents, Maria and Oscar, had gone to bed. It was Thursday night and on the horror channel they were showing '80s horror flicks. Tonight they showed Kurt Russel's classic, *The Thing*. With his eyes glued to the screen, Jared munched on some popcorn that was in a bowl that sat on his lap. Butter melted on top of them.

Someone pulled down on the door handle and opened it. He expected his mother to be standing there complaining about the TV being too loud. Catching the remote, Jared lowered the volume but stopped when he realized nobody was standing outside the living room. Putting down the bowl, he stood and glanced up the hallway to see if either parent had gotten up.

Their bedroom door was closed and it looked like no one had been walking about.

Remembering what happened last time something like this occurred, Jared walked into the kitchen.

Standing over by the window was the mysterious woman in her light blue dress. She stared out into the horizon, her eyes fixated on some anonymous thing.

Jared exhaled a deep breath, plucking up the courage to speak.

"Excuse me, ma'am. Why are you here? What do you want me to do?"

Turning around she faced him, this time with an even grimmer expression than before. "Beware."

"Beware what?"

"Death is coming." The mysterious woman faded until she had completely disappeared, leaving Jared to wonder who exactly was going to die: him or someone he loved?

PART TWO: RUN, TITUS, RUN!

Jared slipped on a blue face mask as he stood outside the cafe. Adrian had texted him earlier to meet up. This was a welcome distraction from what was going on at home with that mysterious lady appearing with ominous messages.

After opening the door, he quickly surveyed the diner. Relaxing jazz music played in the background. A fresh smell of varnish coming from the gleaming skirting boards assailed his nostrils. Adrian was sitting at the back, reading something on his cell phone. When Covid struck, the restaurant halved the number of tables to ensure social distancing. Jared ordered a strawberry sundae and started for Adrian's table.

As he got closer, he noticed that his friend's black curls were now replaced by a mohawk.

"Hey, Jared, man," he said, swiping the screen to lock it.

"Whoa, look at you! What did you do to your hair?" he joked.

Slipping the phone into his pocket, Adrian answered. "I needed a change. It's good to see you. Damn, lockdowns are a pain in the ass."

"Tell me about it. Pity it only ended yesterday. When do you go back to college?"

"Tomorrow," Adrian said, his head lowered in both disappointment and regret.

"That sucks."

"I know, but what can you do? So, what've you been up to?"

"Not much, just studying and binging on Netflix. You?"

"Busy with college. My physical therapy course is great."

"How are you and Tina?"

"We're good. She's texting me all the time. I'm meeting her later tonight to see a movie."

"Is that all you're meeting up for?" Jared asked with a mischievous grin.

"Well, we'll see, won't we?" Adrian replied with an equally devilish smile.

A server arrived with the strawberry sundae. Jared thanked him. It looked delicious, with a single slice of strawberry embedded sideways into the spiraling mountain of cream wobbling on top.

Jared scooped up some off the top, tasting it, moaning with satisfaction. "Now that's a good sundae," he remarked.

"What about your love life? Seeing anyone?" Adrian asked.

"My *love life*? Non-existent, bro'."

"Give it time. It'll happen. You hear from Jess lately?"

"Yeah, she emailed me last week. She's doing good. Her mom is still sober and she's loving college."

"That's cool. Really glad things are working out for her." Adrian took another sip of his coffee. Jared could tell from his friend's semi-concerned expression that he wanted to ask him a question.

"Got something on your mind?"

"Guess your aunt taught you mind-reading tricks too, huh?" Adrian smiled, shifting uncomfortably in his seat. "Have you been experiencing any more strange...stuff?"

"Well," Jared leaned in closer, lowering his voice, "there has been this lady appearing to me recently. I mean since last year I've been seeing them more often."

"By *them* you mean...?"

"Ghosts? Uh-huh. Anyway, this one is different. I don't know what it is but she gives off a kind of weird vibe."

"Weird, how?" Adrian was no longer slouched, he sat up straight, his curiosity piqued.

"It's hard to say...kind of like she's missing something and wants it back. But last night..." Jared's voice trailed off, not knowing whether to continue. He lowered his eyes, unable to meet Adrian's gaze of growing concern.

"What happened last night?"

"She said...," Jared cleared his throat. "She said someone's gonna die."

"What?" Adrian said, an octave higher than normal. "Did she say who?"

"No dude. Just that 'death is coming', or something like that."

Both boys sat in silence. Jared could see from Adrian's blanched face that those words were sinking in.

"So that could be anybody?"

"Yup." Jared continued eating his dessert.

“What did she look like, this ghost?”

“Kind of like those chicks in the cowboy movies except she was black. Don’t think she’s from around here. She sounded French. I kind of feel there was something powerful about her.”

“In what way?”

“It’s hard to say exactly. I think she might’ve been a witch.”

“Oh great,” Adrian said. “Did you do a Google search on her?”

“How can I? I don’t know who she is.”

Adrian downed what remained of the coffee. “Change of plans. Come over to my place and we’re gonna find out who this ghost is.”

“Hold up, you’re meeting Tina later.”

“If someone’s going to die, I’m gonna do all I can to make sure that doesn’t happen. So meet me at my house in about two hours?”

“All right, cool. Thanks, bro’.”

“See you then.” Adrian went to the counter to pay for his coffee.

Jared didn’t know if the Google search would prove useful but he was glad Adrian was helping him. His friend found out that it was Caleb Hammerson haunting them last year through an internet search. Jared hoped this search would be fruitful as well.

***

Zane splashed some cold water on his face in the men’s restroom at work. He’d felt sluggish all day and was not moving as fast as he usually did. Spending another sleepless night in the car had zapped a lot of his energy. Zane’s back and legs ached from the way he slept. Adding to his misery while stocking a shelf, he’d dropped a jar of pickles earlier, which had shattered and spread out all over the floor. His boss, Mr. Roberts, threw him a look that screamed the next mishap would come out of his paycheck.

For an hour, Zane sat at the checkout scanning through people’s groceries. He preferred doing this type of work because it didn’t involve much lifting. So far in his eight-hour shift, he had drunk three cups of coffee. When Mr. Roberts told him that more shelves had to be re-stocked, the need for one more cup overcame him.

Sitting in the small dining area opposite the deli, Zane drank his coffee and ate a chocolate eclair which oozed fresh cream. This brief respite gave him the energy boost that was needed, banishing tiredness and sluggishness for now.

Halfway through stocking the shelf, Zane nervously eyed a crate containing jars of chopped carrots. The fear of dropping something else still hung over him.

Really hope I don't mess this up, he thought.

After ten minutes of carefully placing each jar behind one another, only a few remained. Just as he picked the next one up, a familiar sound caused an icy chill to surge down his spine. It was a low growl coming from a dog. Zane jumped in surprise...and dropped the jar of chopped carrots. This dog's growl sounded very familiar, though Zane hadn't heard it for a long time. He turned around expecting the animal to be standing there, frothing at the mouth. Instead, the aisle was empty.

Mr. Roberts arrived seconds later with a face red with anger, shooting Zane a thunderous look. "What's wrong with you today?"

"Sorry, sir, I didn't sleep well last night," he answered sheepishly, his head lowered in shame.

"Get your crap together, Zane." Pointing to the carrots spread out on the floor, he continued, "Clean it up before somebody falls and hurts themselves." The man started walking away when he stopped and turned back briefly. "Oh, and that's coming out of your paycheck."

Wonderful, Zane thought, heading to the storeroom to fetch a mop and bucket. Telling his boss the truth wasn't an option. Besides, who'd believe that he heard a dead dog anyway?

Eight Years Ago

Zane got out of the car and waved goodbye to his mom before she pulled away. He then turned to Reggie who sat at the bus stop.

"You ready?"

"Hell yeah." They high-fived one another before going to Jackie's Diner. Zane knew both his parents were at work so they wouldn't catch him skipping school.

“Today’s gonna be epic,” Reggie said.

“I hope so. Still not sure about this.”

“Aw, come on, Z. Relax man. We’re gonna be fine. Chill.”

Zane walked a little faster to the diner hoping that nobody would notice them.

The boys sat down and ordered two milkshakes but Reggie wanted a chocolate cheesecake with his. A Christina Aguilera song played in the background. The powerful aroma of coffee invaded their nostrils.

“So, did you see Spartacus last night?” Reggie asked.

“Uh-huh. Sure did. Those fight scenes were sick.”

“See all that blood when Crixus hacked off the soldier’s arm?”

“I laughed out loud when I saw that.” Both boys chuckled at the comment. In Zane’s peripheral vision, he could see two ladies sitting opposite them wearing bemused expressions, giving looks of disapproval.

“Are you getting the next GTA when it comes out?”

Reggie was about to answer when the server arrived with their order.

“Sure am. I’ve been saving up for it for a few months.” *That cheesecake looks nice*, Zane thought, instantly filled with regret. He took a sip of his milkshake.

When another customer walked in, his eyes widened in horror. The tall imposing figure of Mr. Hammond, his next-door neighbor, had entered. A dark gray baseball hat covered his bald head.

“Oh crap.” Zane put a hand up to his face, keeping it low, trying to hide.

“What’s wrong?”

“Old Man Hammond just came in.”

The man placed his order and started walking in their direction in search of a seat.

“Damn, he’s coming down,” Zane said, panic creeping into his voice.

“Just chill,” Reggie replied in a low tone.

As Mr. Hammond was about to pass them, he stopped, taking a step back. “Zane, is that you?”

Shoot! "Oh, hi." The boy gave him a brave smile, trying to conceal the trepidation he felt.

"You boys got school today?"

Zane was about to answer when Reggie butted in. "We got a few free classes until lunch."

"Okey dokey." Mr. Hammond nodded, believing the boy's explanation. "Well, enjoy your shakes."

"Thanks, we will," Zane replied with a nervous laugh.

"See, that wasn't so bad, was it?" Reggie said, taking another mouthful of the dessert.

"If it's okay with you, can we just finish these and go to the arcade already?"

"You really need to relax." Reggie exhaled a sigh of frustration before continuing. "Fine, if it makes you feel better, we'll go now." Wolfing down the rest of the cheesecake and drinking his milkshake in record time, he wiped his mouth on his sleeve. "Happy now?" he asked in an annoyed tone.

"Yup. Let's go." Zane gave a quick worrisome glance to his neighbor who was busy reading a paper. *Just hope he doesn't meet Mom or Dad.*

An hour later, Zane and Reggie were in the middle of a bout in a fighting game.

"Get over here!" Zane said, mimicking his chosen fighter, delivering a jaw-breaking uppercut.

Reggie's ninja jumped back up, somersaulting over another harpoon attack. Mashing the buttons, Zane's character performed the signature freezing move, showering the character with some ice. Reggie finished the bout with a sliding attack.

"Damn, I was *sooo* close to winning this time!" Zane whined.

"Told you I'm the best at this game."

"Yeah, yeah." Zane rolled his eyes, hearing it for the tenth time today.

Within an instant, Reggie's smug grin evaporated.

"What?" Zane asked, noticing his friend's sudden change.

"It's your mom."

"Zane Arthur Miller," her voice carried over the sounds from other video games. The brunette stood with a hand on the left hip, her brows knitted together in ire. "What the hell do you think you're doing?"

Busted. He didn't answer, instead averting his eyes to the ground in humiliation.

"Get your butt in the car. Now! You too, Reginald."

"I knew this was a bad idea," Zane grumbled.

"Shut up," Reggie shot back under his breath.

Both boys picked up their bags and marched out, ignoring the smirks from a few others who were there.

"Be glad your father isn't here," she said as they walked out the door. Margery dropped them off at school, this time staying in the car until they both went in.

Zane sat at the table alone in the cafeteria, coiling spaghetti around a fork, waiting for Reggie to join him. Margery's ear bashing from earlier still lingering in his mind. Had it been his dad who collected him, it could've been so much worse. Zane shoved the plate away, the thought of food no longer appealing to him.

Reggie, carrying a tray filled with a large hamburger on a plate and bowl of green Jell-O, pulled up a chair. "You okay, dude?"

"What do you think?" Zane said flatly.

"That good, huh?" Reggie's lips curled, but when there was no reaction but a serious expression, his smile faded. "Do you think your mom will tell on me?"

"Maybe, maybe not. Who knows? Bet I know who ratted us out, though."

"Who?" Reggie took a bite of the hamburger.

"Old Man Hammond. Had to be. He's the only one who saw us."

"We don't know that for sure." Reggie swallowed the hot food. Unscrewing the cap off a bottle of water, he drank some, quenching the heat burning his throat.

Zane, with folded arms, met Reggie's eyes in a stern stare. "Can you think of anyone else who'd do it?"

"Well…no."

"There you go. He's not going to get away with this."

Reggie wiped his mouth and put down the burger. "Whoa, remind me to never piss you off."

"Sorry. I'm just mad at him."

"Kind of noticed that. So, what are you gonna do?"

Zane gave a dismissive wave. "Nah, forget I said anything."

"Are you worried about your dad finding out?" Zane's silence acted as confirmation. "Don't. I'm sure your mom's not gonna tell him."

"Sure hope not," Zane replied.

Later that day, the two boys stepped off the bus. Reggie's mother waited for him in her silver 2005 Lincoln.

"Text you soon, all right?" Reggie said.

"Sure." Zane began the fifteen-minute walk to his house. Margery wasn't there to collect him because she knew that he'd come straight home.

Just as he was passing Mr. Hammond's gate, the old man, trimming the overgrown bush raised his head, seeing the teenager passing by.

"Hello there. Have a nice day at school?"

"Yeah, real swell," he said sarcastically.

"Got busted, huh? It never pays to skip classes. Once you go down that road, you're on a slippery slope."

So it was him! "How did you know I was skipping school?"

"I was young once, too. We did it a few times, me and my friends. My pa had my hide the last time. I swore never again."

Zane was about to ask if Mr. Hammond had ratted him out but it was clear from the man's tone that he had.

"Guess you'll know better next time, right?" He almost sounded like he was gloating, but the old man's expression was deadpan.

"Yeah, sure." As Zane walked away, he thought, *You're so gonna pay for this.*

Three hours dwindled by and Zane was unable to complete the homework, his mind consumed with revenge. Picking up the cell phone, he tapped Reggie's name. He answered after three rings.

"What's up?" Reggie said.

"Well, did your mom say anything?"

"Yeah, your mom told mine what we did. I'm grounded for three weeks."

Zane rolled his eyes heavenwards. He felt his face turn scarlet with embarrassment. "I'm sorry, man."

"Don't be. We knew the risks."

"Still…" Zane's eyes fell on the elderly neighbor's house. "I definitely know who squealed on us."

"Let me guess, it was Mr. Hammond?"

"Of course it was. He practically admitted it to me." Zane talked about the conversation he had with him earlier.

"That sucks. Why did he do that?"

"Because he's a jerk, that's why."

"Funny, I always thought he was a nice guy. So, what d'ya wanna do?"

He watched as Mr. Hammond's beige pug, Titus, came out of his white kennel. "Think I have an idea. I'll tell you tomorrow at school."

"So you're really gonna get even with him?"

"Hell yeah." The sound of someone coming up the stairs made him finish the call abruptly. "I gotta go. Bye." Closing the flip phone, he placed it on the desk.

Two years before, Mr. Hammond had complained about Reggie and Zane skating around the neighborhood on their skateboards. After the seventh complaint, Margery had enough and confiscated Zane's. He swore that if the old man did something else to him ever again, it would be payback.

Now it was time to make good on that promise.

***

Zane waved goodbye to his parents as they drove off to meet some work pals for a barbeque. He was grounded but that fitted into his plan. A few days ago, he found out that Mr. Hammond would be gone for a while on Saturday to compete with the local bowling team in a national tournament.

For an hour or two Zane sat alone in his room, waiting for the man to leave. Now the time had come and a roguish smile spread across the boy's face as Mr. Hammond, holding his bowling bag, locked the front door and left when a friend picked him up.

"Good, he's gone. Now to have some fun." Zane, in a covert manner like a silent commando climbed the wall, quietly dropping into his neighbor's backyard.

Titus, sensing Zane's presence, began barking. Walking out of the kennel, he sniffed the air, turning in the boy's direction. The dog panted while walking toward him.

"Hey Titus. Who's a good boy?" Zane rubbed him down, making the dog at ease while surreptitiously slipping the extra-long chain off his collar.

Eyeing the black side gate, Zane pulled back its bolt. From his pocket, he took out a piece of bacon wrapped in tissue. He threw the meat to the other side. He knew Titus was watching him and waited for the dog to follow the bacon's scent. He grinned as Titus pushed back the gate before eating the meat.

Time to go. Zane climbed the wall and sat on top of it, watching Titus run free from Mr. Hammond's yard.

Let's see how you like that, he thought while jumping down into his own garden.

As he locked the back door, there was a loud screech of a car in front of the house. Running out, he stopped in his tracks.

There, standing outside a cream-colored 2012 Subaru, was a distraught middle-aged female driver close to tears, staring down at something.

Oh no, please don't let it be— Too late. It was. Titus lay on the ground, all life drained from his eyes. "Dream a Little Dream of Me" played on the radio of the woman's car, escaping through her rolled-down window.

"Oh my God," was what slipped from Zane's mouth as he watched on, ashen-faced. *I never meant for him to be killed. I just wanted him to run away.*

Now it was Zane's turn to be distraught as he ran to his bedroom.

What have I done? Forever he'd have that gruesome image of Titus lying on his side, blood flowing from his mouth and ribcage. A white piece of bone protruding through beige fur.

In the days that followed, Zane heard that Mr. Hammond asked if any neighbor saw someone suspicious around his home. Nobody did and no one suspected Zane of being guilty in freeing Titus. Night after night for weeks, guilt wrecked him and he couldn't sleep. Several times Zane came close to admitting what happened but couldn't. He dreaded his father's reaction and thought he might go to jail.

On Thursday afternoon, a week after Titus's death, Zane was in the kitchen preparing a peanut-butter jelly sandwich when Margery's phone conversation with a colleague caught the boy's attention.

"Yeah, that was awful what happened to poor Titus. Richard isn't sure how he broke free." There were a few "uh-huhs" and perfunctory nods in response to what she was hearing over the line until she spoke again. "I totally agree. The world's gone nuts. Speaking of nuts, did I tell you what my little sunshine did a few weeks ago?" There was a pause. Zane suspected she hadn't. "Well, he and his friend thought it would be a great idea to skip school." Again, another pause. "I know. Totally brazen! They would've gotten away with it too if not for Kathy from HR. She saw them and texted me."

Zane gripped the counter, suddenly overwhelmed with a wave of weakness, both knees threatening to buckle underneath him.

So, Old Man Hammond didn't rat on me, and Titus was killed for nothing!

His stomach churned; food was the last thing he needed right now. Abandoning the sandwich, he rushed up to his room to spend another night crying, with that sickening feeling swirling around him, driving the stake of guilt even more into his heart.

Present Day

Zane sniffled while lying back in the seat of his car. Many times over the years he tried to make it up to his neighbor, mowing his lawns, driving him to wherever he needed to go, or even getting groceries when the man couldn't. Nothing he did made it right or erased the large lump of shame that was forever lodged in his throat.

***

Zane rang Reggie's doorbell. Feeling the stubble on his face made him wish he had shaved earlier before coming here, especially if Monica was inside. Monica's home was a two-bedroom apartment. He admired her decorative taste, the bright vibrant peach paint in the hall, and the living-room painted a lemon yellow. On a sunny day, the room lifted his mood as the walls seemed to glow from the sun's rays pouring in. Some paintings adorning the walls were quirky yet stylish, leaving one to stare at them and wonder what it was they were actually looking at. Yet there was something elegant about them, giving the place a touch of class. Zane had always wanted to be a painter but lacked the talent.

Reggie opened the door. He held a bottle of beer.

"Hey bud," Reggie greeted him. Then his smile disappeared. Zane knew it was because of his shabby appearance. "Whoa, everything all right?"

"Just not been sleeping well."

"Is that all?"

"Are you gonna invite me in or are we gonna talk about it out here?" Zane joked.

"Oh, sure." Reggie stepped back, opening the door even more.

Zane entered the apartment. On an old-style mahogany table in the hallway was an incense burner. Small plumes of smoke rose from within it as an incense stick burned, releasing a soothing oceanic smell. That was another trait about Monica's home, it was always welcoming and relaxing, two things he missed from his own right now.

"So what's up?" Reggie asked while closing the door.

"I've not been sleeping well. Just...got a lot on my mind."

Reggie raised his bottle. "Want a beer?"

Tempting as it was to drink one, he didn't want to risk being pulled over by cops.

"I'm good," Zane replied, shaking his head. He was so tired, that even one sip would get him drunk.

Both men entered the living room and sat down. Some reality TV show was on. Reggie pressed a button on the remote to mute it.

"How's work? Did you just come from there?"

"Yeah, and it kinda sucked today. I dropped two jars."

"Oh. Bet Roberts wasn't too happy about that."

"Nope. Not one bit. Said the second one's coming out of my paycheck."

Reggie whistled in amazement. "I knew the guy was a bit of a slave driver but didn't think he was an ass, too." He took a swig from the bottle.

"Yeah, well, guess I gotta be more careful in future. Where's Monica?"

"In the shower."

Zane absorbed the room again, staring at every piece of furniture and painting. "You're lucky, you know that, right? You've a nice place, a hot girlfriend. Guys would kill for that."

Reggie smiled as he answered, "Is someone a little jealous?"

With a flush creeping across his cheeks, Zane cast his gaze to his feet. "Maybe. But seriously, Reg, you got it good. Don't mess it up."

"I won't. Where's all this coming from? I know you're tired but what aren't you telling me?"

"Nothing. Just been doing a lot of thinking lately about the past. I—"

Monica shutting her bedroom door, made Zane stop. As she walked into the room, she gave him one of her friendly yet seductive grins. "Hey."

"Hi." He tried with all his might to keep his eyes focused on a painting, and not roving over her body.

"Can I get you something, coffee, soda?" she asked.

"Already offered," Reggie jumped in.

"No, I'm good, thanks."

Reggie waited until Monica had gone into the kitchen. Zane felt his friend's gaze fall upon him, knowing that something wasn't right.

“Tell you what, why don’t I come over later and we can talk then? I can bring a few brewskies. How does that sound?”

“Cool. Only if that’s okay with Monica. I don’t wanna interrupt your plans.”

“She’ll still be here when I come back. Besides, bros stick together.” Reggie offered his clenched fist in a knuckle bump. Zane bumped it.

“See you later. Bye, Monica.” He got up and left.

***

Jared shut Adrian’s front door. Part of him felt nervous about searching for this ghost woman. There was no guarantee that they could even find her. What if they found out her true identity and it caused something terrible to happen? Would another spell of bad luck come upon them? All these thoughts ran through his mind while walking to Adrian’s room.

“Hi Jared,” Don called out. Jared didn’t see Adrian’s dad at first but heard his voice coming from the kitchen.

As they entered the room, he came into view. “Oh, hi, Mr. Cole,” Jared replied.

“How’s college treating you?” Don sat at the table, eating a salad.

“Good. I’m off for two weeks.”

“Enjoying the break?”

“Yeah, sure am.” He felt bad lying but Don wouldn’t understand. Adrian didn’t tell his father the whole truth about what had happened last year, only that Maybelle had cleared some negative energy from the house.

Hell, even I still can’t believe what happened. Ghosts come to me for help. How messed up is that? Despite his incredulity, Jared embraced his new role and wasn’t fighting it any longer.

Making his way to Adrian’s room before Don could ask any more questions, he shut the bedroom door. It had changed little. The desk with a laptop and his mom’s picture beside it was still in front of the large window. Some stationery and a notepad were just below Mrs. Cole’s picture. Two shelves containing fantasy novels were over his bed. He placed DVDs on top of his wardrobe. Next to them was a small TV set that had a DVD player built into it.

"Thanks for doing this. I hope Tina wasn't too mad."

"No, she's cool about it."

"Still didn't tell her the whole truth about last year yet, huh?"

"No, not yet. So, where do you think we should start?" Adrian's reply was a sign that he didn't want to talk about the exorcism at the well. Much like Jared, he probably still had nightmares too.

"That's the thing, I don't know. She didn't give me her name."

"Okay, let's approach this a different way. What was she wearing?"

"Like I said, one of those dresses you see in those cowboy movies."

Adrian grabbed the notepad and a pen. "So she's 19th century." He jotted the observation down. "The lady is black. What age do you think she was?"

"Mid-forties maybe."

"You said she sounded French?"

Jared nodded.

Adrian scribbled down that fact also. "What was her hair like?" Jared explained how she had her hair tied up in a bun. "Did she wear anything that stood out?"

Jared closed his eyes again, remembering the first time the woman appeared. The dress was what he remembered first, then the long hair. On her left index finger was a ring. "She had a gold ring on a finger on her left hand."

"Describe it."

In his mind Jared pictured her again, this time zooming in on the gold piece of jewelry. It was like a triangle within a square, two lines going diagonally on either side. Jared told Adrian what he saw and his friend wrote it down.

"Let's see what we get here." Adrian opened up a new tab on his browser. He typed in Jared's description of the symbol. Several images appeared. "Any of these look familiar?"

As Adrian scrolled halfway down the page, an image stood out. Although it was a faded, grainy black-and-white photo there was no mistaking that symbol.

"There, that one." Jarod pointed to it.

Adrian clicked on the picture. A side window appeared with some text underneath it. Both boys read what was on screen. Jared gulped and his heart beat a little faster.

"It's some kind of voodoo symbol," Jared said, trying not to sound scared.

"That's a good thing."

"It is?" Jared answered surprised. "Since when is voodoo a 'good thing'?"

"Since it might tell us more about this lady," Adrian replied confidently, altering his search words to "Voodoo priestess in the 1800s Hopps Town".

"Wait a sec', how do you know she was a priestess?" Jared asked.

"I don't, but it's worth a try, right?" Hitting the return key, a whole new slew of images popped up. One called to Jared the most.

There, standing outside an old makeshift hardware/grocery store was the woman with her arms folded. A wicker basket containing food and other items sat by her feet.

"That's her, that's the one." Jared tapped on the picture twice.

Adrian clicked on the image. It took them to a site run by a voodoo practitioner. On the site's voodoo history page, it showed the black-and-white picture again with a caption underneath it.

"Madame Freya Farooq," Jared said while reading the name. He continued, "Freya was the first voodoo priestess to come to Hopps Town. In the early years, she practiced it in private with only a select few." Jared stopped reading; a sudden realization came over him. "Did someone put a curse over us? Is that what she meant?"

"Guess you'll have to ask her next time she appears."

Either way, this is bad, Jared thought. In his opinion, it was worse not knowing what was around the corner or what was coming for him or his friends.

***

Maybelle stared at herself in the mirror as she dried her long hair that she loved to have dreadlocked. Recently she'd decided on crochet braids for a change. She felt refreshed after the shower, relishing the water bouncing off her mocha-brown skin. It had been a stressful day at the call center with phones ringing non-stop. Her arm and wrists were sore from typing furiously while replying to customers' questions. Now her pains had eased from the hot water from the shower. Maybelle had started the new job a few weeks ago, quitting the administration position in the old daycare center. She loved kids but not her boss and his constant criticisms or put-downs.

After putting on her pajamas, she paused. A cool air invaded the room, making the hairs on her arms tingle. Maybelle saw something pressing down on the mattress, sitting on the other side of the bed.

Jumping up, she turned around, ready to face whatever was there.

"Ma," Maybelle barked, nettled. She pressed a hand to her chest, "I hate when you do that!"

"Sorry honey," her mother chuckled. "It never gets old." Hyacinth Duval was still in the black silk dress she had been buried in, her salt and paper hair neatly tied up in a braided bun.

"Well, I'm glad you think it's funny," Maybelle snapped, inhaling and exhaling a deep breath, letting her heartbeat return to normal.

"I may be dead, child, but your old mama still likes to have fun." Her beaming smile waned. "But this isn't a normal visit. I'm here to deliver a message."

"What message?" Maybelle's brows narrowed in concern.

"Something's going down in Hopps Town and Jared's gonna need your help."

"Can you be a bit more specific?"

"Jared's about to bite off more than he can chew, so he's gonna need your guidance. That's all I can say right now."

"Is he in trouble?" Maybelle sat on her bed again.

"He will be if he tackles this problem alone. You need to go to him. As in, *right now*."

"I can't just up and leave like that. What about work?"

"Child, blood's more important than a damn job. That boy will be in a world of hurt if he does this alone. Go there tomorrow." Hyacinth stood up, facing the wall. She walked toward it and stopped, turning back, "You're his mentor like I was yours. He needs you. Do what God put you here to do." She walked through the wall.

"Guess I'm going to Hopps Town." Maybelle sighed, took out a suitcase, and began packing.

***

Zane opened the door when the bell rang. Reggie stood there with a six-pack tucked underneath his left arm.

"You brought the goods. Cool," Zane said.

"I never come empty-handed," Reggie replied, making his way to the living-room, putting the cans of beer on the table.

Zane got two glasses from a cupboard in his kitchen. He put one in front of Reggie and sat down in a chair opposite him.

Reggie noticed the DVD cover of the first Avengers movie on the couch. He stared at Scarlet Johansson in her black, skin-tight leather costume. "She's hot, huh?" he said, nodding his head at the actress.

"I guess she's all right."

"Come on. You're telling me you wouldn't tap that?"

"As if I'd ever have a chance anyway," Zane scoffed.

"Good point." Reggie opened up a can. "So, what do you wanna talk about?"

"It's probably nothing. Just stuff from the past coming up," Zane replied as he poured some beer into his glass.

"No offense, but you can't BS me, Z. I've known you since we were kids." After taking two slugs, he continued. "Something's up. What's wrong?"

Zane put down his glass. "I've been having these weird experiences. Like earlier today at work, I thought I heard Titus barking."

"*Titus*? As in Old Man Hammond's dog?"

"Yeah."

"But that mutt's dead."

"I know, that's what makes this thing weird." Zane picked up the beer and drank some more.

"So you're telling me you're hearing a dead dog barking?"

"It sounds crazy—"

"Well yeah," Reggie laughed incredulously.

"It *happened*, Reg," Zane replied firmly.

Motioning for calm with both hands, Reggie said, "All right, I believe you. Really, I do. When did this all begin?"

"About a week ago. Everything was fine before that and then bam! All this crazy stuff happens." Zane noticed Reggie's eyebrows raise in shock and his face blanched. "What? Is there something *you're* not telling me?"

"No, everything's cool with me. Can I use your bathroom?"

"Sure," Zane replied, his voice trailing off in concern.

Reggie put his glass on the table again and went to the bathroom.

Reggie sat on the toilet. What Zane was experiencing began around the same time he had that strange incident where something stroked his hair. Reggie wanted to open up about it but couldn't. Part of him knew that if he did, he'd have to acknowledge that it was real. The other part of him didn't want to make Zane even more scared than he already was.

Should I tell him? Poor guy must be going crazy. Reggie thought about it for a few more moments, deciding not to say anything.

He flushed the toilet and washed his hands. Bending down in front of the sink, Reggie splashed water on his face. It felt uncharacteristically warm even for cold water.

"Whoa!" Reggie gasped, backing away from the sink. "What the fuck…?" His heart pounded in his ears.

Blood ran from the faucet, painting Zane's white, pristine ceramic sink red.

Reggie watched it sluice off his fingertips.

With trembling hands he turned off the faucet. Reggie snapped some toilet paper off the roll, drying his fingers and the droplets that fell on the floor. He dried each finger carefully and got some more tissues. As he was about to dab them in the sink, he noticed that there was no trace of blood left. Taking a quick glance at the tissues in the restroom used to clean his fingers, they were devoid of any crimson.

What's causing all this? Reggie thought and secretly wished it would stop.

Pressing his back up against the wall, Reggie controlled his panicky breathing, taking a few deep breaths, reminding himself to calm down, at least for Zane's sake.

Just as he was about to return to the living room, Zane's bedroom door was ajar. It was open wide enough for Reggie to see something glowing in a drawer inside one of the bedside lockers. Quickly stepping inside, Reggie opened the drawer and saw a pocket watch. It radiated a white, ethereal glow.

At first, he staggered back, eyes blinking rapidly, trying to process what he was seeing. Then slowly, Reggie approached it. The ethereal glow had vanished. "What the..." He picked up the watch, opening it. "This is the one he showed me in the store."

"Reg, you okay?" Zane called out.

"Yeah, will be up in a minute."

Suddenly he winced, muffling a scream by covering his mouth. The silver object sizzled on his left palm, leaving an imprint. Throwing the watch back into the drawer and closing it, Reggie rushed to the bathroom and ran cold water on the burn, quenching the stinging pain.

Should I tell him what just happened? he thought while still running water on his hand. *That thing could be cursed. Maybe that's what's causing all this weird stuff.* After drying his palm and wrapping tissue around it, Reggie decided not to.

Stuffing the injured hand into his left jeans pocket, he returned to the living-room. "I gotta go. Monica just texted me; she forgot her key."

"Oh, okay," Zane said with disappointment.

"We'll pick this up another time, right?" Reggie opened the front door. "Look, I really gotta go. Talk later." Leaving, he rushed to his car.

Inspecting the burn again, it looked raw, stinging like hell. *Definitely gotta put some ointment on that when I go home.*

He put his Toyota into reverse and raced back to Monica's apartment.

Twenty minutes later, Reggie stood in his kitchen. "Monica!" he called out. Silence was his only answer.

Good, she's not here, he thought while rushing to the bathroom. Unwrapping the tissue, he saw the burn was an angry red. This was something he didn't want his girlfriend to see. Trying to explain it away would be hard. Flashbacks of blood running from the faucet ruled Reggie's mind, not allowing him to think of anything else.

Gingerly, he placed his burned palm underneath cold water. The cool liquid splashing off the wound stung even more, making him grimace. Drying his hand, he grabbed some ointment from the medicine cabinet. Squirting a thin line on the wound, Reggie massaged it in. For a few seconds, an intense heat grew where the watch marked him until it died down again.

While cradling his hand up to his chest and putting the ointment back in the cabinet, he froze upon hearing a girl giggle out in the garden. Just as Reggie turned around, he caught a glimpse of the tail end of a young girl's blonde hair passing by.

"Hey," Reggie shouted. A few months before, some young teenagers had broken into Monica's garden, jumping a fence he had erected to keep them out.

Damn kids are back again, he thought while racing out the backdoor to investigate.

Standing in the middle of their garden, Reggie scanned his surroundings. There were no footprints in the grass. Nothing seemed disturbed, no deckchairs overturned or anything out of place.

With his burned hand still held up, Reggie was about to go back inside when more giggling came from behind the wall at the side of their apartment.

Got you now, Reggie thought, running to the wall. Peering over it, his face turned pale. Once more, nothing was there.

This crap's happening again! With one last sweeping glance, Reggie darted inside, locking all doors.

Leaning up against the bathroom wall, Reggie took two drops of an herbal remedy on his tongue. Monica used this to get rid of all nervousness before an interview. Now he needed it too. After a few minutes, his heart, which had been threatening to leap out through his chest, slowed down. The herbal remedy had kicked in.

After wrapping a fresh bandage around the wound, Reggie was about to leave when the sound of laughter made him stop again. This time it sounded slightly older, like a teenage girl, and more familiar as well. Too familiar. He dared not turn around. Sweat eked out through every pore in his body.

The girlish laughter came closer to the window until it was directly outside. It ended when something smacked off the window. Reggie jumped. Mustering all his inner strength, he pivoted, one step at a time.

He recoiled, bumping off the door when he saw what was on the glass.

A bloody handprint. Beside it, scrawled in blood, were two words: "*Miss me?*"

***

Jared had just turned off the lawnmower when a car honked twice while entering their driveway. He turned around and saw that it was Maybelle. With a beaming smile and eyes wide in delight, Jared went over to greet her.

"Hey Belle," he said. She waved back from inside the car with a jubilant smile of her own.

Then a frightening thought struck him. *Is she here because something bad's gonna happen? Is this all connected to Madame Farooq?* He hid his worries by acting naturally, opening the door for her, still beaming.

"Hi, baby, good to see you again," Maybelle said, getting out of the car. She hugged him tight. "Have you grown?" Maybelle asked taking a step back, eyeing him up and down.

"Maybe a few inches."

"You're getting more handsome every day."

"Do you want me to bring in your bags?" Jared said, standing by her trunk, ready to open it.

"No, I'm not staying here. I'm at a B&B in town."

"Oh, okay. For how long?"

"Why, you trying to get rid of me already?" Maybelle joked.

Slanting his body away in embarrassment, Jared said, "No."

"Relax. I don't know how long I'll be here. That depends." Before he could ask what she meant by that, his aunt continued. "I'll explain later. Come on, let's go inside to mom and dad."

While Maybelle was talking to Oscar and Maria, Jared noticed her watching him like she did last year, observing his every gesture, trying to see if there was anything wrong. This made him certain that something was definitely happening and she hadn't just come for a social visit.

An hour later, Maybelle had to leave to get a few things for her stay. Just as she was about to pull out of their driveway, she beckoned Jared over to the car.

"Yeah Belle?"

"Do you wanna have breakfast with your favorite aunt tomorrow morning? It's on me."

"Uh, cool. Yeah, sure. Maybe then you might tell me why you're here? I'm guessing it's to do with ghosts and stuff?"

"So you've mastered the Jedi mind-reading trick?" They both laughed and she winked at him. "Don't worry, I'll tell you everything. See you at ten."

"You got it."

Maybelle reversed out, heading up the road into town.

***

Gunshots from a cop show on TV awakened Zane. He had fallen asleep on the couch. Pulling up his sleeve, one look at the watch revealed that it was 11pm.

I gotta go to bed, he thought, knowing that an early start awaited him.

After washing his face in the bathroom, he entered his bedroom. His room wasn't as large as he'd wanted, but still wide enough to fit a dressing table and two wardrobes. Two months ago he had painted it a pale blue. On the walls were a smattering of family pictures and one large photo of a wounded Jesus hanging on the cross that Margery had forced upon him. This hung directly across from his bed.

Just as Zane was about to turn off the bedside lamp, growling from outside the bedroom door made his blood turn cold.

Oh no, not again. He reached for the baseball bat angled against his bedside locker. Someone or something pushed down the handle on the bedroom door twice.

Zane jumped up on the mattress, his baseball bat at the ready. Standing out in the hallway with tire marks over his pudgy body was Titus, teeth bared, saliva dripping from his mouth.

"Get away from me," Zane shouted, his hands and lips trembling.

Titus, still growling, entered the room, taking one slow step at a time like a tiger circling its prey. His eyes were as dark as coal. The dead dog first walked to the left of the bed and then right, never averting his eyes from the target.

"I'm sorry, okay! Is that what you want me to say? I'm sorry. There. I said it," Zane yelled, both palms moist from sweat. His mouth was dry.

Titus stopped at the foot of the bed and though his growling ceased, those razor-sharp teeth were still bared, hungry for a taste of blood. Taking several steps back, Titus ran and jumped onto the mattress.

"Oh crap," Zane yelped. "Get away!" he roared, this time swinging his bat. He missed intentionally, hoping to warn the mutt off.

His attacker was unfazed, taking another step closer instead.

Zane retreated another two, now meeting a dead-end with his back pressed up against the wall.

Titus' eyes narrowed and growled again. He knew Zane had nowhere to go. The pudgy dog crouched down into a leaping stance.

"It's gonna jump for me," he muttered, now ready to bash Titus. Moving back two paces, the dog barked twice before running at Zane.

Letting loose a feral scream, Zane closed his eyes and swung the bat, not wanting his last image to be Titus biting him. For a few seconds, he waited to feel sharp teeth penetrate his flesh, tearing into bone. When nothing happened, Zane opened both eyes only to see that he was alone again, with a fresh, warm pee stain on his briefs.

Dropping the bat, Zane sunk to his knees, bawling. It had been a long time since he cried like this but all that had occurred over the last week was finally taking its toll.

Why is this happening? While drying his eyes, he stopped sobbing as something even more peculiar grabbed his attention.

Light crept out from a drawer that contained the pocket watch.

What the...? He cautiously reached out to open the drawer. Once opened, he withdrew his hands. White rays of light rose and fell. Moving a little closer, Zane peered in to see bright hues pouring out from the watch's engravings. Part of him wanted to touch it.

"Not a chance," he said, kicking the drawer closed again. Soon the strange illumination dimmed, then disappeared. "Could that be what's causing all this?" He thought about it for a moment. These bizarre occurrences had started after the watch first came into the house. Then it all made sense, every part of the puzzle fitted together.

That thing is cursed! No way Mom's getting it now. There wasn't much use in bringing it back to Stevenson's Pawn Shop, Zane reasoned because he'd never get a refund. Neither did he want anyone else to suffer because of whatever supernatural power was in it. The thought of throwing it into a river came to him, but if someone went fishing they might catch it.

Apart from, *How can I get rid of that thing?* One other thought remained: why was he seeing Titus after all these years?

***

That same night, Reggie sat at the late-night diner, a warm cup of coffee keeping him company. Earlier he texted Monica that he'd be late, working at the garage. It was easier to lie than tell her what was really causing him to stay away from their apartment. The blackness of his coffee resembled what Reggie felt around him. When Zane told him about what he was going through, he knew that now was the perfect time to reveal the torment currently ripping his peaceful world apart.

Today, they elevated that torture to a whole new level.

Reggie began work as usual, checking the roster and list of chores to be done. While fixing a carburetor he dropped a wrench. When he bent down to pick it up from underneath the car he saw a girl enter the main office.

"Hey, you can't go in there," Reggie shouted.

She shut the door, ignoring his calls.

Putting down the wrench he marched toward the office. Opening the door to shout at whoever had wandered in, he stopped short when he saw there was no one in the room. Only a pink scarf laying across a chair. Picking it up, he brought it out into the workshop area.

"Hey, any of you ladies drop this?" he asked the two female mechanics. Both shook their heads.

Reggie brought it back in, searching the backroom. Nothing. Bringing the scarf up to his nose, he caught the scent of something from his past, from someone he once loved.

No, it can't be, Reggie thought.

Putting the scarf in the lost and found drawer, he walked out.

Just as Reggie was about to leave, he saw something from the corner of his eye that made him pause.

Taking a step back, he forced himself to turn his head to what was on one of the CCTV monitors that was switched off. Staring back at him was what looked like the reflection of a pale 15-year-old blonde girl of medium height in jeans and a ripped, blood-stained pink sweater. She had cuts and bruises on her face.

Reggie recoiled and spun around to face the specter, but whatever was with him had disappeared. He knew all too well who it had been.

For the rest of his shift he couldn't concentrate. The haunting image of that girl seared into his brain, making it difficult for him to focus for the rest of his shift. A few times he had to start something from scratch because of losing concentration. His co-workers noticed he was spooked and expressed their curiosity and concern through their stares, but they refrained from asking what was wrong.

Now the prospect of driving home and possibly encountering that girl again, made Reggie want to delay the inevitable. Deep down, he knew Monica would be concerned if he stayed out any later. After knocking back the rest of his coffee, he left the diner.

Switching off the engine, Reggie killed the headlights, staring blankly at the apartment's front door.

"Can't stay here forever," he muttered.

Closing the door gently, he popped his head into their bedroom. Monica was on her side, sound asleep.

Sitting at the kitchen table, Reggie stared at a bottle of beer he took out from the fridge. Touching the cold glass brought him a sense of comfort, keeping his mind on the present and not what occurred earlier.

"Are you okay, honey?" Monica's voice made him jump. He hadn't heard her getting up.

"Uh, yeah, sure. Just a long day. Did I wake you?"

She pulled up a chair, sitting beside him. "No, I needed to pee and saw the light on. Reg, I know something's going on and it frustrates me you're keeping me in the dark. Why aren't you telling me what's happening? Are you in trouble?"

"No... it's complicated."

"Then *uncomplicate* it for me," Monica demanded.

"I don't know where to begin."

"Usually from the start helps," she replied, her answer combining anger and sarcasm.

"Do we really have to do this now? Can't it wait until tomorrow?"

"And tomorrow you'll blow me off again." Monica lowered her tone, putting a hand on his. "I'm just worried about you. By not knowing what's going on means I can't help. You're my world, Reg. You know that, right?"

"Of course." He squeezed her hand and gave her a weak smile. "It's just weird and...and I don't know how to explain it." Reggie sat in silence staring at the beer bottle again.

"Fine, tell me tomorrow." Monica got up, pushing in the chair a little too hard, rattling the table. He knew that this was her way of letting him know she was mad as if the stomping off to their room wasn't clear enough.

Tomorrow I'll have to tell her. I can't keep her in the dark any longer.

Scrolling through his X feed, Reggie raised the bottle to take another swig of beer but paused. His jaw hung open in horrified awe.

An outline of a face formed on the wall opposite him. He took a quick glance at his bottle and wondered if the drink was tainted.

Reggie squinted again. The outlining of the face was still there, its cheekbones and eyes were forming. He wasn't imagining it. Now a nose was added.

Reggie jumped up from his chair.

A mouth appeared and then long hair. The figure was an almost transparent gray but easy to distinguish a face belonging to the girl he saw earlier today.

The rest of her body formed on the wall. She sprouted from it, like a sheet enveloping her.

Just as Reggie was about to flee, the kitchen door slammed shut, trapping him. "Monica. Open the door! Get up!" he screamed, pounding it, tears blurring his vision.

The sound of Monica running from their bedroom brought little consolation. "What is it, Reg?" she yelled. Despite twisting the handle left and right, it wouldn't budge. "Open the door, Reggie!"

"I can't. It won't let me."

"What do you mean?"

His answer was abruptly cut off by a soft voice humming a tune behind him.

Reggie turned around to watch the ghost stepping through the 'sheet' that enveloped her, the girl's body no longer a monochrome gray.

"Oh, Jesus!" Reggie frantically twisted the handle and shook the door. "Help me, Mon!"

"What's happening?" she cried.

Fingers drummed on the table.

"Heya Reggie," the girl said.

This isn't real. This isn't real, was the mantra he tried to use to convince himself that this was all an illusion.

"Oh Reggie-kins," the girl called out in a sing-song voice.

Reggie stopped trying to make himself believe it wasn't real. Instead, he mustered up all his courage to turn around and face his ghostly tormentor.

"Did you tell her about me?"

Reggie didn't answer. With one large gulp, hoping to get rid of the lump in his throat, he faced her.

"Wha— why are y-you doing this, Lisa?" he asked.

"Oh, so you *do* remember me," she replied, her arms folded, an eyebrow arched in bemusement. "You know, the girl you supposedly loved once. The one you left to *die*!"

PART THREE: HAUNTING MEMORIES

Seven Years Ago

Sounds of machine-gun fire, explosions, and crowds cheering in various shoot 'em ups and sports games swirled around the arcade. Seventeen-year-old Reggie pummeled buttons as he tried to string together a killer six-hit combo. Sweat trickled down his forehead as he was moments away from victory. Just as the final blow was about to be delivered, the opponent blocked it, striking one of his own. It was game over.

"Aw damn," Reggie moaned, before scooping up more quarters from his pocket. *I gotta have one last try.* Slipping two into the machine, he picked a different character.

After winning the rematch, grinning from ear to ear, he felt confident facing his next opponent. That confidence was short-lived as his character faced a brutal beating without being able to strike once in reply.

Guess it's time to call it quits. Reggie backed away from the game, surveying the others around him, deciding what to play next. Despite having a console at home, he loved to get out of the house, away from his overbearing father, listening to lectures about poor grades and being a 'loser'. This was one thing both he and Zane had in common: a dislike for their fathers.

Shouts of joy from the next machine put a brief halt to his search for a new game. Taking a peek, he saw a girl playing *Space Invaders*, demolishing all her enemies with pixelated beams. He eyed her up and down. She was the same height as him, in navy shorts and a blue sweater. Bleached blonde hair fell halfway down her back. Soon, she was overtaking the highest score with every level she passed.

"Wow, you're good," he remarked.

"Thanks," the girl replied, pounding a button to fire more beams from the spaceship, moving the joystick left and right to avoid being blown up. Upon passing the level, the game played a piece of retro music.

"Do you come here often?" Reggie said.

"Really? You're going to start with the cheesiest line of all?" she answered with a mischievous smirk while massaging her wrist.

"No, I didn't mean—"

"Chill. I was just kidding. I come here a few times a month, just to get out. Know what I mean?"

Tell me about it. "Yeah, I understand. Let me guess, your dad?"

"No, not that it's any of your business." This time there was a slight harshness in her words.

Reggie eased off on the questions. "Okay, sorry. I wasn't trying to be nosey or anything. I'm Reggie."

"Nice name." The new level began with more space creatures zigzagging down the screen. She pushed the buttons, killing all the aliens.

"Guess you like the classics, huh?"

"Me and Dad used to play it when I was little. Why? Do you think it's lame?"

"No, I'm just more of a *Street Fighter*, *Tekken,* and *Mortal Kombat* guy."

"I saw that. Pity you sucked." Reggie regarded her with a frown until she turned around with an attractive smile, revealing perfect white teeth, giving a quick, "I'm kidding" before focusing on passing another level.

"Boom!" she said minutes later, with her left hand raised in triumph. "Game over."

"Those guys didn't stand a chance," Reggie remarked.

"Nope." She blew both her hands as if they were hot smoking guns. "These are mean, lean killing machines." Both teenagers laughed at her comment.

"So, what are you gonna play next? D'ya wanna play me in something?" Reggie asked.

Taking out a cell phone, she checked the time on it. "Sorry, I gotta go. I'll be grounded if I get home late. Another day?"

"Umm...sure. Same time next week?"

"Got it," she said while walking. At the door, she stopped and said, "Oh, my name's Lisa. See you next week, Reggie."

"Looking forward to it," he said as Lisa left.

***

Present Day

Reggie stumbled out of the kitchen into Monica's arms.

"What the hell happened in there?" Monica shouted.

He couldn't answer, still in a daze, panting, sweat running down his back.

"Look at you, you're white as a ghost. Tell me what happened!"

"Something…on the…wall," he blurted out, still trying to catch his breath.

"What was on the wall? You're not making any sense, Reg." Monica held onto him, studying his face.

"I gotta…" Pointing to the bathroom, he staggered more than walked there.

"All right, but don't be long. We need to talk about this!"

Reggie slumped against the bathroom door, panting and speechless. His chest rose and fell. Sweat patches were on the back of his t-shirt. Lisa had vanished, but her words still rang in his ears.

Steadying his trembling hand and getting a firm grip on himself, Reggie stood up. Splashing some water onto his face, and after washing his hands under the shiny silver faucet, Reggie dried them with an orange towel. Monica's dad re-decorated the bathroom with dark teal tiles on its walls, and white tiles on the floor. Over the sink was a mirror with a mirror light, which could be turned on by pulling a cord.

Just as he was about to leave, a faint sound caught his attention. It was indistinguishable and came from outside the window.

"Not again..." Standing by it, Reggie strained to hear the sound once more. Now it became clearer; a voice, increasing in volume. A girl called out something in a sing-song tone.

He froze when what the girl was saying became less muffled. She was calling his name...now coming from within the sinkhole.

Reggie bent over, moving his ear closer. Once more, his name was called.

While retreating to the wall, part of him wanted to run. Something, maybe pure curiosity, made him stay to see what happened next.

More eerie, indistinct whispers came from deep within the sinkhole, soon swirling around the bathroom. With his eyes darting around every corner of the room, he made for the door.

Just as he was about to dash out, two hands shot out from the wall, grabbing his arms and pulling him back.

"Help! Get off me!"

"Miss me, Reg?" the girl asked.

Monica pounded on the door while shouting, "What the hell's wrong?"

Fingers with long, claw-like nails gripped his ears. They penetrated flesh and bone, threatening to tear his ear off.

Reggie screamed as he wriggled and tried to force himself free. Blood began oozing out of where the hands gripped him. More and more he could feel it separating from his head.

Once Monica realized someone had opened the door, she rushed in.

Lisa's hands vanished.

Reggie backed away from the wall, panting, feeling his ear, each fingertip devoid of any blood.

"Jesus, Reg, what happened?" Monica demanded to know while hugging him.

"Noth— nothing, babe. I just thought I felt something in my ear."

"I'm not buying that. This is the second time tonight something freaked you out! Come on, tell me."

"Remem—" Reggie's lips trembled; his face still white. "Remember...Lisa?"

"Yeah, the girl who died?"

He nodded. "Well, I know this is gonna sound crazy but..." A lengthy pause made Monica grow even more frustrated.

"But what?" she said, her voice raised a fraction in annoyance.

"She's been haunting me for the last week."

Monica was speechless for a moment. He could see by her observing his body language that she was looking for obvious signs that he was joking. There were none.

"Wait...you mean, she's *here*?" Again he nodded, still unable to say too many words. "Why now after all these years?"

He shrugged his shoulders, "I— I— do—don't know. There's more."

"More?" Monica replied, her voice raised a little higher in horrified astonishment.

"Yes..." Reggie's eyes fell to his feet. He swallowed hard, finding words to describe what he needed to say next. "Apparently, Zane is going through some stuff, too."

"As in... ghost stuff?"

"Uh-huh. A few days ago I called over and he told me that he's been seeing a dead dog. I went to the bathroom at his house and I saw this old-fashioned watch in his room. I mean...it was glowing...like really bright."

Monica raised her left eyebrow, tilting her head to the side. From her semi-stone-faced expression, Reggie could see that part of her didn't believe what he was saying. "Where was it in his bedroom?"

Taking a deep breath, Reggie braced himself for the backlash when he said, "In his drawer."

"You went through his damn drawers?" Monica barked.

"I didn't mean to, it just kind of...called to me."

"Geez, Reg." Monica threw her hands up in the air, shaking her head in disbelief. She waited a minute to calm down. "What happened then?"

"I went to look at it. The watch burned my hand." He held it up, still bandaged. "Since then, things have gotten weirder. I think that thing is cursed."

"Well, is she here now?" Reggie shook his head. "Did you tell Zane about the watch?"

"How could I? What was I supposed to say? 'Oh, by the way, Zane, that watch you have in your drawer is cursed.'?"

"Maybe not like that...you told him about your experiences, right?" Reggie bowed his head. Silence confirmed that he didn't. "You gotta tell him. The poor guy must think he's going crazy!"

"It was hard enough telling you."

"You need to phone Zane. Right *now,*" she insisted.

"Okay, okay. I will." He threw some water on his face, dried it, inhaling a few deep breaths to compose himself. He reached inside his pocket for the phone and pressed Zane's name on the contact list. After a few rings, his friend answered.

"Hel— hello," Zane stuttered in a shaky breath.

"Is something wrong, bud?"

"I can't take much more of this," Zane answered, sobbing.

"Calm down. Are you hurt?"

"No... just freaking out, man. That thing attacked me."

"I'm coming over."

"We're taking my car. You're in no state to drive," Monica said.

Fifteen minutes later, they arrived. Zane's door was slightly ajar. Reggie shot his girlfriend a look of concern before entering.

"Zane...where are you?" Reggie called out.

"In here," a voice called out from the back of the apartment.

"You better stay outside," Reggie warned Monica before going further. His eyes scanned around the hallway and living room, hoping nothing would jump out. He stopped outside the bedroom.

"Can I come in?"

"Yeah," Zane answered.

Reggie pushed the bedroom door open, staying expressionless, trying to hide his astonishment. Zane was curled up on the bed in the fetal position, eyes red from crying.

"Christ, Z." Reggie stepped in, sitting down on the bed beside him. "What the hell happened here?"

Zane never lifted his head to meet his friend's gaze, instead opting to focus on the wall. "Titus, that's what."

"Did he...just appear out of nowhere and come at you?"

"More or less."

"And then what?"

"He jumped to bite me and I swung the bat. Next thing I know...he's gone."

"You can't stay here tonight. Come on, you're coming with me." Reggie picked up Zane's pants, handing them to him.

"No, I can't. I just wanna be alone."

"It's not safe, Z. What kind of friend would I be if I left you here?"

Zane sighed before sitting up. "You sure?"

"Certain. I can't leave you here like this."

"Thanks," he said meekly, his ears red with embarrassment while taking the pants. "There's something else I wanna say, too."

"What's that?"

"I think that watch I got for my mom is cursed."

"Okay, look we can talk about that tomorrow. Let's just get out of here."

A minute later, all three were in the car, driving back to Monica's apartment.

***

The next morning, Reggie and Monica sat opposite Zane at a booth in Jackie's Diner. He had dark circles around his eyes and stubble on his jaw. Reggie, dressed in his blue work overalls, knew his friend was going through hell. Now it was time to let him know he wasn't the only one.

The server arrived with two coffees and a mocha latte for Monica.

"Thanks," Monica said, sliding a coffee to each of the two men. The server placed the bill on the table.

"Yesterday you said you wanted to talk about the watch, but, Z, there's something I gotta say."

Zane took a sip of his drink. "What is it?"

"I wasn't exactly telling you the truth about what was going on with me. I've been having weird crap happen in my place too."

Zane paused to bring the cup to his lips as he looked at Reggie with eyes full of incredulity. "What kind of *weird crap*?"

"I've been..." Reggie hesitated a moment, still trying to come to terms with it himself.

"Yes...?" Zane said, eager to hear the rest of that sentence.

"I've been seeing Lisa for the past week."

"Wait…as in dead Lisa?" Reggie nodded the affirmative. "Wow."

He could see a wave of relief washing over Zane's face. "I wanted to tell you sooner but when I saw you freaking out, I didn't want to make it worse."

"And you say this has been going on for the last week?" Zane asked.

"Uh-huh but like I said, I didn't want—"

"To freak me out, yeah, I know," Zane interjected. "And you think this is connected to the pocket watch?" Zane interjected.

"That's what we're getting to," Monica added. This time her tone was insistent as she glared at her boyfriend while continuing, "Reggie has something else he wants to say. Don't you?"

Reggie gave her a 'thanks-for-throwing-me-under-the-bus' look. "Yes…um…don't get mad at me but when I used your bathroom a few nights ago, I saw something in your room. The pocket watch in your drawer was—"

"Let me guess, glowing?"

Reggie and Monica sat there in stunned silence until Reggie broke it. "You know?"

"Only found out last night. Like I said, I think the damn thing's cursed."

"Me too." Reggie refrained from telling him that the watch burned his hand. "Ever since I saw it, Lisa's been appearing often. She's more vicious."

"Sorry to hear that. Don't know what I can do with the watch, though." Zane gazed hopelessly into his cup, steam rising from the coffee. "It was a gift for my mom, but I can't give it to her now. If I throw the damn thing away, someone else might find it and be cursed, too."

"Where did you get it?" Monica asked.

"Stevenson's Pawn Shop."

"Maybe he might know who had it before you?" Monica suggested.

"He wouldn't tell me," Zane replied.

"Mon's right. He might say who had it last. Worth a shot."

Zane shook his head. "Stevenson won't tell me. Besides, what would I say if he asks why I wanna know? He'd laugh me out of the store if I told him the truth."

Monica reached out, squeezing his hand in support. "Don't

worry. We'll figure something out." She drank some of her latte.

"Did Lisa say anything to you?" Zane asked gingerly.

"She still blames me for her death. Maybe this is some kind of revenge. I don't know."

"Either way, what happened seven years ago wasn't your fault. You gotta know that, right?" Zane reminded him.

"I know, but she doesn't see it that way," Reggie replied.

"How do we know it's even her? It could be some demon or something," Monica suggested.

Both boys looked at her with semi-incredulous expressions.

"Hey, I watch *Paranormal Witness* too. Just saying." Monica drank the rest of her latte. "Like I said, don't worry. We'll figure something out. You're welcome to stay at ours tonight if you want?"

"Thanks but no, running away isn't the answer either."

"Come on, I'll drive you home." Monica picked up her handbag and grabbed the bill. "It's on me."

"You guys are great."

"Wouldn't have it any other way." She turned to Reggie and said, "You staying?"

"Yup. Gonna just have one more coffee before I start work."

"'Kay, catch you later." She kissed him before sliding out of the booth.

"We'll speak again soon," Zane said. Just as he was about to turn to walk away, he stopped. "Oh, and stay out of my drawers," he said with a wink and half-grin.

"Gotcha," Reggie replied. They knuckle-bumped before Zane left.

Speaking about Lisa and their time together brought up an old memory that haunted him a lot longer than the girl's spirit.

Seven Years Ago

Reggie sat outside the arcade where he had met Lisa two months before. When she met him that second time the following week, they learned a lot about each other. They had a lot of similar interests and liked the same TV shows, books, and movies. A few days after that meeting, both met up again. And it was on that date that they kissed.

Reggie felt like the luckiest guy in the world to be going out with such a pretty girl.

"Hey Reggie-kins," Lisa said as she got off her bike, leaning it against the wall.

"Hey there," he answered, waving back.

She removed her pink helmet and they kissed. "Ready to go get that soda?"

"I've been looking forward to it all day." He held her hand as they walked into the diner.

For half an hour both teens sat, enjoying their sodas, talking about the latest episode of *Revenge*. A tall, bulky, raven-haired man in a red leather jacket and brown jeans entered. Two of his friends came in a few seconds later standing behind him, waiting to order something. One had a dark navy baseball cap and a scruffy goatee. The other had tattoos of skulls and various guns up along his left arm.

Reggie didn't recognize them but didn't like the vibe they gave off. There was something untoward about these men. The two behind Red Leather Jacket Man wore torn t-shirts. One guy had ripped jeans, the other dirty gray sweatpants. They all looked like they were in their early twenties.

When Red Leather Jacket Man looked directly at Reggie, he froze. Nothing but menace lurked in his eyes.

"Lisa, we better go."

"Why?" she asked, confused. "We're having a good time here."

He didn't take his eyes off the three strangers.

Lisa noticed him staring at someone behind her and turned around. When she saw them, she turned back.

"You're right, let's go." Lisa finished the soda and grabbed her coat.

Just as they were making their way to the door, Red Leather Jacket Man saw her approaching. His eyes lit up. "Well, hello, doll."

Lisa tried to pass him but he stood in front of the door. "Where ya goin'? I just wanna talk is all."

"I don't, so excuse me." She opened the door but the man closed it shut again.

"Now that ain't polite. Your mama never teach ya any manners?"

"Sir, we wanna leave so let us pass," Reggie said.

Red Leather Jacket Man eyed him up and down in disgust. "Why you with a little twerp like him when you can have a man like me?"

"Umm...let me think. Maybe because he's not a creep and you are."

Reggie grinned at Lisa's remark, but when he saw anger flare in the goon's eyes he stopped.

"You think something's funny, boy?" Red Leather Jacket Man asked.

"N— no," he stammered.

"Think he needs to be taught a lesson, Vic," Scruffy Goatee said.

"Looks that way, don't it, John?" Vic moved in closer to Reggie's face. His acrid breath reeking of beer and cigarettes was now only mere inches away. "How's about me and you step outside?"

"Not interested," Reggie replied. This time he tried to open the door but Vic closed it again.

"Vic, Rick, whatever your name is, this is getting old. Let us go, you jerk," Lisa shouted.

"Everything all right here?" a server said, throwing a wary stare at the men.

"Everything's peachy," Vic answered, stepping aside.

Lisa and Reggie rushed out the door.

An hour later, they were lying on the grass in the park, staring up at the cloudless sky. Reggie could see from Lisa's pale complexion she was shaken up. He was too and tried to mask it behind a brave face, cracking some jokes about the incident. Right now though, they were alone.

Lisa gazed at him and chuckled.

"What?" he asked.

"Nothing. I just love looking into those green peepers of yours."

"Why?"

"Just do."

A strand of blonde hair fell loose from Lisa's hairband. He put it behind her ear. "Yours aren't half bad either."

She leaned in, kissing him.

"Got some more of that to go around, honey?" a familiar menacing voice said.

They got up as Vic and his two friends approached them.

"Come on, we're leaving," she said. Reggie picked up his coat; she, her bag.

The two other men blocked their path to the bikes.

"Aw, where ya goin'? We just wanna have fun," Vic said. His friends sniggered.

"We're not interested," Reggie spoke up.

"Think you're a big man, don'tcha?" Vic presented him with an intense stare for a few seconds. He flinched as the older man feigned a punch. All three thugs laughed at Reggie's response.

"Look, we just wanna go home. Let us get our bikes and we'll be gone," Lisa pleaded.

"Thing is, sweetie," Vic now stood in front of her. She arched her back a little as he tried to stroke her cheek. "I don't want you to go." He pointed a dismissive finger at Reggie, "You can leave but you, darlin'," now pointing at Lisa, "Well, I can think of a few things we can do."

In a moment of frustration, Reggie snapped, pushing Vic away. "Back off." Instantly he regretted it when Vic pulled out a pocket-knife, popping its blade. He snarled,

"You stupid, son of a—"

"Do you want our money?" Lisa interjected. She opened her bag, pulled out a wallet and threw it to the ground. "Here, take everything I got."

Vic glanced at the wallet and laughed. "Boy, you're a true blonde, ain't ya?"

"I know what you want, perv'," Lisa's left hand reached into the bag, "and it's not on the menu!" She quickly took out a can of mace, spraying it into Vic's face.

The man screamed, dropping the knife, clutching his eyes.

"Run!" Reggie screamed. They bolted, abandoning both bikes.

Reggie heard the two men gaining on them. Vic continued to roar as mace stung him.

"Come back here," John shouted, sounding four to five feet away. Their panting was getting closer.

Reggie's heart almost stopped when he heard Lisa fall. The other man grabbed the girl, getting on her back and pinning her down.

"I got the bitch, Vic," he cried out, spit running down his jaw like a ravenous dog.

"No!" Reggie halted, standing his ground.

John chasing him threw a punch.

Reggie ducked and sucker-punched him in the mid-region.

Howling in pain, John doubled over.

The frightened teen rushed to Lisa, shoving Vic's other buddy off of her. Grabbing the girl's hand, he pulled her up.

Together they ran toward the cobbled path leading to the park's exit.

"Come on, Lis, we're almost there," he shouted, his girlfriend lagging him but he could still see her in his peripheral vision, sweat and tears running down her face.

A gunshot shattered the park's silence.

Reggie heard Lisa fall behind him again. He skidded to a halt, a hand raised to his mouth.

"No!" he bellowed as Lisa lay face down, moaning and feeling her side, her fingertips moist with blood.

John held a gun, its metal body glinting in the sunlight. A trembling hand steadied its aim, now directly pointing at Reggie.

Torn between staying with Lisa or running for his life, Reggie's survival instincts kicked in. He ran. Tears of guilt for leaving her behind flowed down his face. Any second now he expected another gunshot to ring out, a bullet to rip right through his body.

"You idiot," he heard Vic yell at John. "She ain't much good now."

Up ahead, he saw a police unit parked opposite the exit. Reggie bolted for the car, screaming for the cops' attention as he got closer, praying that it wasn't too late to get Lisa some help.

Present Day

Reggie furtively rubbed a tear from his eye as he was back in 2020 again. After he had reached the police officers, they radioed in an ambulance and rushed to where Lisa lay but it was in vain. The bullet hit a major artery and she bled out, despite an officer putting a towel up against her wound to prevent blood flowing out from it.

Three days later, the authorities caught Vic and his friends. That brought little solace to Reggie and Lisa's family.

For years, many 'what if' questions ran through his mind. Night after night he lay awake, wondering what would have happened if he had stayed. Deep down, Reggie knew he had done the right thing by getting help. That didn't ease the pain or pangs of guilt that assaulted him all these years.

As Reggie wiped at another tear that was about to roll off his cheek, a server passed by.

"You okay, sir?" she asked, noticing him crying despite his best attempts to hide it.

"Yeah, I'm good."

"Want some more coffee?"

"Nah. I gotta get to work anyway."

She nodded, moving on to clear a table.

Reggie wedged a five-dollar bill underneath a saltshaker before getting up to leave. Now that Lisa was haunting him, he pondered on how to make her stop.

***

"You go on ahead and I'll be down in a minute," Maybelle told Jared. "The usual?"

"Yup," he replied. Jared found a seat at the back. Part of him was relieved to have Maybelle here because it meant that whatever he was dealing with, it didn't have to be faced alone. He just hoped that she'd stick around long enough to confront whatever Madame Farooq had in store for him.

Maybelle sat down, putting the handbag over her chair. "So, how ya doing?"

"College is going okay."

"Love life?"

"You're the second person to ask me that since I came back. Don't have one."

"Come on, there gotta be some guy you like."

"Gotta be honest with ya, Belle, after Tim died last year, I haven't been lookin'."

Their coffees arrived. They both thanked the server.

"So, why are you really here in Hopps Town?" Jared asked.

"I sense something's going on or going down. Am I right?"

"Uh-huh, except I don't really know what it is."

"Tell me what you *do* know." Maybelle took a sip of her coffee. Wincing at how bland it tasted, she tore open a packet of sugar, tipping it in.

"It all started when I saw this lady in our kitchen over a week ago."

"What did she look like?"

It was Jared's turn to take a sip of his coffee. "That's hot." He poured some milk in, stirring it before continuing. "She looked like one of those ladies from cowboy movies."

"So she was from the 1800s?"

"Uh-huh. But it gets weirder. Adrian helped me look her up online. Turns out she was a Voodoo priestess or something."

"Voodoo?" Maybelle said, creases now forming on her brow.

"Told you it was creepy. She wore this ring and it had a kind of symbol on it, a Voodoo symbol, I think."

"Did you get a name?" Maybelle drank some more.

"Madame Farooq. She started the first Voodoo group in Hopps Town in the late 1890s. I think there's one still here."

"Jared, Voodoo is nasty. You don't wanna mess with that stuff."

"Damn straight. You don't have to tell me twice. Thing is, she said something like 'Death is coming' and that they took something from her."

Maybelle fell silent for a moment after hearing this. "Did she say who took what from her and who's gonna die?" Jared shook his head. "We need to find out what it is and fast. Maybe she wants it back and won't rest till she gets it."

Jared asked the question that popped into his head since they began this conversation. "Who told you that something was going down here?"

Maybelle was about to answer when she paused, staring beyond him.

"What?" he asked.

"The answer is standing by the door."

He turned around to see only a handful of diners at different tables eating their food. "I see nothing."

"Look again. This time, focus."

The boy turned in his seat, staring at the door. Shutting his eyes for a moment, he took a deep breath, exhaling it slowly. Jared opened them. Hyacinth was standing at the diner's entrance. Seeing her again filled him with joy. She smiled and waved at him. He waved back, quickly forgetting where he was.

Hyacinth walked towards him and stood beside a young man in his early twenties with a ponytail.

"This guy needs your help," Hyacinth spoke to both Jared and Maybelle. "He and his friend are in way over their heads. If something isn't done and soon, they'll both be dead by the end of the week."

There were so many questions Jared wanted to ask her. Like, 'Are you okay?' and 'What's it like over there?' Deep down he knew she didn't have time to answer all those so he wanted to try asking something telepathically. *What kind of trouble are they in and why do you think we can help?*

"That's something you two have to figure out on your own. All I can say is that evil is around something his friend has and now him. I've come to point you in the right direction, child. You two take the reins from here." Hyacinth gave the man a look of sympathy as if she were feeling his pain. "Don't take long or it'll be too late." Hyacinth waved goodbye before vanishing.

Jared swallowed the mixed emotions he had upon seeing his grandmother, fighting back tears by reminding himself of the job at hand. Hyacinth was like a second mother to him, always giving sound advice and baking his favorite apple pie, cutting him a slice every Saturday when he called. *God, I miss her.*

"You okay, J?" Maybelle asked as if sensing his sadness.

"I'll be fine." Jared leaned in, whispering, "So how do we do this? I mean, we can't just walk up to him and say, 'Hey, my dead grandma said you need our help'."

"Let me do all the talking." Pointing to his cup she concluded, "Drink up. I've a feeling this could be a long day."

"That's if he doesn't tell us to get lost."

"This ain't my first rodeo. I know how to handle people."

Jared finished the coffee. "Lead the way."

The mechanic placed some money under a saltshaker and stood up to leave.

Maybelle approached the young man's table. "Hi."

He regarded her with some suspicion and confusion. "Hi..." His voice trailed off in uncertainty.

"My name is Maybelle and this is my nephew Jared."

The mechanic nodded his head in greeting. "What can I do for you, ma'am? If you've come about a car, I'm just about to start my shift."

"I'm not here about that. Look, I know what I'm about to say will sound crazy but just hear me out."

"Okay..." Once more he eyed them both, now with a bit more nervousness.

Jared could tell from his facial expression that the mechanic was thinking of running from the diner.

"Me and Jared here have special...gifts."

"What kind of, 'special gifts'?" His posture went rigid accompanied by an unimpressed expression.

"We're able to see the dead," she replied.

"Wait a second, if you're trying to sell me a palm reading, I'm not interested."

"It's nothing like that, I promise," Maybelle answered.

"Did Zane put you guys up to this?"

"I'm guessing Zane is your friend, the one who's in trouble?" Maybelle asked.

The mechanic folded his arms. "Well, you're the psychic, you tell me."

"Sir, I know this all sounds insane but despite what you think, we are here to help."

"My aunt is right. Your friend has something that could get the both of you killed." When Jared said this, the dismissive expression and body language were relaxed.

"All right, I'm listening."

"Can we sit down?" Maybelle said, pointing to the chairs. The mechanic nodded. All three sat down. "Do you mind if I ask what your name is?"

"Reggie. Now tell me about Zane."

"Jared, do you want to start?"

He shifted in his chair uncomfortably, coughing twice before talking. "About a week ago I first started seeing this lady named Madame Farooq. She was a Voodoo priestess. She told me something was taken from her and if it's not given back, bad things will happen."

"What kind of *bad things*?" Reggie asked.

Jared hesitated in answering for a moment, exchanging a nervous glance with Maybelle, not really sure of how to break it gently. "Well um...I think somebody's gonna die...and soon."

Reggie's arms were now unfolded. "And Madame...whatever told you this?"

"No... but she implied it."

Maybelle jumped in. "So then my Ma who passed, came to me in spirit and told me I needed to come here to help Jared sort this. Then she appeared here just a few minutes ago and said we need to help you and Zane."

"I... I don't know what to say. I mean, put yourself in my shoes. If someone came up to you in a diner and said all this, what would you think?"

"Man, I dig what you're saying. If it were me about thirteen months ago, I'd be skeptical too but Belle and I are telling the truth."

"And I think a part of you knows we are," she added.

Reggie was silent for a moment. Jared could tell by the man's pensive expression that he was weighing everything up in his mind.

"And how can you help me and Zane exactly?"

"If Zane gives us whatever he has that's causing all this, we can take it back and carry out a ritual to make all these hauntings stop. I know you guys are seeing and experiencing stuff, right?"

"Yeah, we are." Shoving up the sleeve, Reggie's watch revealed that he was nearly ten minutes late for work. "This is a lot to take in. I have to think it over. Do you have a card?"

"No, but I can give you my number," Maybelle replied.

"And let's just say I believe you, and Zane's on board with you helping us, how much is this gonna cost?"

"We don't charge," Jared answered. "We do it cos we want to."

"God gave us these gifts for a reason. We use them to help people, plain and simple," Maybelle added.

Reggie sat back, stretched his arms while staring up at the ceiling, mulling everything over. He sighed before giving in. "Give me your number and I'll talk to Zane. If he's okay with this, we'll be in touch."

"Works for me." Maybelle opened her handbag, took out a notepad and a pen. She jotted down the cell number, writing her name over it. Tearing the page from the pad, she gave it to him.

"Thanks." Reggie folded the paper up, putting it in a pocket in his overalls. "I gotta go. Thanks again." Reggie shoved in his chair and left.

"That went well. At least he doesn't think we're completely nuts," Jared said.

"For his sake, I hope he calls."

"Me too. I got a feeling that things are about to get worse before they're better."

"You're right." Maybelle watched Reggie walk to his car. "But we've done our part. It's all up to them now."

***

After meeting Maybelle and Jared in the diner, Reggie could not think about anything else for the rest of the day. He couldn't get them off his mind no matter how hard he tried. Listening to Radiohead or other rock bands didn't banish the conversation from his thoughts. It lingered like a foul odor.

Driving home from work, what Maybelle and Jared told him again took center stage.

Maybe they overheard Monica saying it to a close friend? Reggie dismissed that thought because she'd never betray his trust by discussing a private matter like that with someone else.

They could have overheard Zane talking about it on the phone. This wasn't beyond the realm of impossibility as Zane could be forgetful of where he was when talking on his cell. One time he told a crude joke to Reggie while standing in a line at a movie theater, not realizing a middle-aged woman and her two grandkids were standing behind him. She cleared her throat in a bemused manner to make him aware of her presence. Reggie always grinned when remembering that.

Or maybe they're for real and want to help. Reggie knew that this was a high possibility because Maybelle and Jared seemed sincere. *We got to do something and fast.*

Pulling into one of their allotted parking spaces outside Monica's apartment, Reggie switched off the engine. Taking out his phone, his finger hovered over Zane's name.

They're the only help we got so far, so why not take a chance on them? Reggie reasoned before tapping his friend's name. A groggy voice soon answered.

"Uh...hello?"

"Hey Z. Were you in bed?"

"Yeah, just catching some shuteye before work tonight."

"I'm surprised you're able to sleep at all after last night."

"It wasn't easy. I hate being here but I don't wanna tell my parents what's going on and it's not fair on you guys me staying there."

"You're welcome any time."

"Roger that. Thanks. Not to sound like a dick or anything but is there a reason you're ringing? What's wrong?"

"Nothing's wrong but I got something you're gonna wanna hear."

***

The next day, Maybelle picked up Jared on their way to Zane's house. Reggie had called late the previous night. He said that his friend wanted to meet up. He passed on the address and she texted Jared.

"Do you think he'll let us help him, Aunt Belle?"

"For his sake, I hope so. It's best I do all the talking."

"Sure thing. You do it better anyway."

Maybelle presented him with a glare, feigning offense. "Are you saying your aunt's a chatterbox?"

"Whoa, no." Jared held up both hands in defense. "I just mean you're better at explaining things. That's all."

"Hmm...nice save." She laughed, no longer keeping the act up. "I'm just ribbing you, J. Relax."

"I know I said this before but it means a lot to me, you being here. I couldn't do it alone."

"Someone reminded me recently that we all need a little help sometimes. But there's gonna come a day you'll have to do this without me."

"Can we not talk about that right now? I mean, we're still in the Luke Skywalker—Obi-Wan Kenobi phase. I'm still in training. Can't imagine myself doing it alone."

"*Star Wars* reference. Nice. You know how to woo a lady," she joked. They both shared a brief guffaw. "Seriously, J, I ain't gonna be here forever but when the time comes, you'll do fine. You already helped a few ghosts without me, right?"

"Yeah but still—"

"But nothing," Maybelle interrupted. "*You* did that. Not me. Don't worry, when the time comes, you'll be busting ghosts or guidin' 'em home."

"Hope I can be as good as you."

"Again with the flattery. Keep that up and I might treat you to burgers and fries when we're done here."

"Sounds good to me."

Maybelle parked the car outside Zane's house. Jared gazed at the man's apartment, studying every inch.

"Are things going to get wild in here?" Jared asked.

"It's possible, so be prepared. If Zane gives us whatever it is he's got, that thing could be hot."

"Meaning...?" Jared asked, his words tinged with an ounce of consternation.

"Meaning it could be possessed."

"And you want *us* to take that away?" Fear was now replaced with exasperation in his voice.

"That's the plan."

"What if whatever is attached to that attacks us?"

Gesturing with her head to the trunk, she replied, "That's why we have the salt and crucifix to make sure that doesn't happen." With one quick glance at Zane's front door, she added, "Come on before this guy changes his mind."

Maybelle knocked on the door. An attractive auburn-haired woman answered it.

"Hi there. I'm Monica. Come in," she said with a friendly smile. They walked in; she closed the door. "Can I get you guys a coffee, soda, or anything?"

"No, we're good, thanks," Maybelle replied.

"This is Zane," Monica said, pointing to her friend.

Zane stood up and shook Maybelle's hand and then Jared's. She introduced herself and her nephew.

"Thanks for coming. Reggie said you can help. Can you tell us how?" Monica asked.

"We'll need to take whatever it is you got that's causing all this. Once we do, we'll keep it safe until we figure out what to do with it."

"Do you want me to get it for you now?" Zane asked.

"Yes please," Maybelle replied.

Zane left, returning a few seconds later. In his hand, he held a shiny old pocket watch.

"Could you put that in a bag?" Maybelle said.

"Um...sure," he replied, his brows narrowed in confusion. He went into the kitchen, returning with the watch in a white plastic bag, handing it to her. "Why do you want it in that?"

"I don't think it's safe to touch it directly just yet," Maybelle said.

"Well, how come I can hold it and not be harmed?" Zane replied.

"It's haunting you and not us. That will change if we touch the watch," Maybelle informed him.

Jared could tell by her face that she was fishing for the words to use for the next question.

"Can I ask what you guys have seen since you got this thing?"

Zane was first to recount his experiences and then Reggie. Jared's jaw lowered in horrifying awe at their stories. Mentally he questioned how these men were still functioning after their ordeals.

And this guy wants to stay here even though all this stuff is happening? Jared thought. *I know I wouldn't. Maybe he got nowhere else to go.*

Maybelle didn't appear shocked. She just nodded every once in a while, taking it in her stride as if she had heard it all before, looking at them with an empathic gaze.

"Wow, you guys have been through the mill, huh?" she remarked.

"Sure have," Zane said. "So now you got the watch, what next?"

"Like I said before, we'll take this home, make it safe. Then we'll find out where it needs to go back to."

Reggie spoke up. "Will you let us know when everything's okay?"

"Of course," Maybelle replied. "I'll be in touch within a few days hopefully."

"Cool. Thanks guys. We appreciate it," Zane said, standing up, shaking both Maybelle and Jared's hands again.

"Yeah, we really do," Reggie agreed.

Jared and Maybelle left the apartment. Maybelle opened the trunk. "Pop the lid off the can of pure salt." Jared did as his aunt asked. She put the cursed object into it.

"What will that do?" he asked.

"It will trap whatever's possessing the pocket watch." She covered the can again, placing the crucifix on top of it. "Father Richard gave that to me."

"The priest who was supposed to do the exorcism last year?"

"Yes, him. He said that was blessed by the Virgin Mary in Medjugorje a few years ago."

"Medjugorje? Where's that?"

"I think it's some holy place in Croatia where Mary appeared every year. Anyway, the crucifix gives us an extra layer of protection."

"So that thing's in jail now, huh?"

Maybelle smiled at his simple but correct analogy. "Yes, it is." She closed the trunk and nodded to the front seats. "Come on, get in." Both sat back in the car. Maybelle continued, "I could kill for a milkshake and a burger. How about you?"

"You buying?"

"Maybe."

"Then I'm in," he grinned while tying his safety belt.

"Being a cheapskate doesn't suit you," she replied with an impish smile.

"My dad said, 'never say no to anything free'."

"Yup, sounds like something he'd say all right." Maybelle started the engine, reversing out of Zane's yard. "Burgers and milkshakes it is, then."

"Did I ever tell you you're my favorite aunt?"

"That wouldn't be too hard since I'm your *only* one."

Jared laughed as they sped away.

***

A day later, Jared arrived at the parking lot of Winslow's Park, half a mile from Hopps Town, named after a Civil War hero, Lt. Gerard Winslow. Maybelle had texted him earlier that morning to meet her there. He knew it had to do with finding out just what exactly did Madame Farooq want with him. Maybe the pocket watch was what she was talking about all along.

Just hope we sort this out soon before somebody gets hurt. Jared got out of the car, pressing a button on his key to lock it.

Maybelle sat on a bench that had a table. In front of her were a coffee cup and a green plastic bag containing bulky items in it. When she saw him, she smiled. "Hey J. You got here early. Good."

"Traffic was light. So how are we gonna do this?"

"Follow me. Take these." She handed him the bag while she carried her coffee. They followed a stone path that led off to the woods.

Being here reminded Jared of the well last year and the creepy forest it was in. Except this one was more alive with different bright orange, green, and yellow autumnal-colored leaves lining both sides of the path.

Maybelle brought him to a clearing where there was a circular patch of land that had no trees. He knew she wanted to do the ritual here so that it would be away from people if anyone came to the park.

"We'll stop here. Give me the bag and hold this." Jared gave it, taking her coffee cup. "Watch and learn."

She took out two cans of pure salt. Opening one of them, Maybelle poured some in a large circle. This would act as a type of wall or force field, keeping out anything bad while they stood inside.

Slipping on a pair of latex gloves, she then took out the pocket watch, still in the white plastic bag and put it on the grass. They poured another mini circle around the pocket watch. Covering her can, she put it on the ground.

"All right, J, you're up."

"What do you want me to do?"

"Center yourself and call on Madame Farooq."

"What will I say if she comes?"

"Tell her we got the pocket watch and ask her if that's what she was talking about. If it is, find out what she wants us to do with it."

"All right. I'll give it a try." Jared centered himself by clearing his mind. Now, all he could hear was his heartbeat and a gentle breeze puffing around him. "Madame Farooq. I need to see you." He waited a few seconds to open his eyes, but she didn't come.

"Try again. Focus harder," Maybelle advised.

Once more, Jared concentrated with both eyes closed tightly, his mind devoid of any thought. "Madame Farooq, please hear me. I need to talk to you."

"J," Maybelle said in a tone that let him know they weren't alone.

He saw Madame Farooq standing outside the salty wall of protection. "Thanks for coming."

"Merci for this," she replied, nodding to the white bag.

Jared pointed to the pocket watch. "Is that what they took from you?"

"Oui."

"Can I ask who *they* were?" Maybelle said.

"Before I moved here from France, Papa gave me that to remember him. That is my prized possession. I met people here. We practiced Voodoo like folks from home did. We made a vow to tell no one, but somebody had a loose tongue. Next thing I knew, wicked men came to the house one night and dragged Madame Farooq from bed. They did," she paused, her breath shaky, "unspeakable things to me...taking turns...."

"Sick pigs," Maybelle said, lowering her head.

Jared knew she felt the woman's pain.

"They turn everything upside down. Wicked men took Papa's watch. Madame Farooq fought back but they slapped and punched me." She stopped, fists clenched, teeth gritted and eyes flaring with anger.

"Before they hang me up on tree like a cochon bled for slaughter, I curse that watch and anyone who had it. Any serious sin they did or guilt they have will come back to haunt and a demon, too."

"Dang, I'm sorry they did that," Jared said.

"So what can we do to make it right?" Maybelle asked.

"Some folk pity me and bury me in grave."

"Where?" Maybelle beat Jared to asking that.

"Old Hopps Town Cemetery."

"I know where it is," Jared said. "If we take back the watch and put it there, will everything be okay?"

"Oui. Hurry. Death come soon for them." Pointing at the watch with her left index finger, she continued, "Once it's on grave, Madame Farooq will restore order." The priestess concluded with an urgent shooing motion, showing they should go. "*Allez*, *allez*!" She shimmered out of view.

"That poor woman," Jared remarked. "Sick sons of—"

"Ah, ah, don't cuss. Gotta watch that tongue."
"Sorry, Aunt Belle."
"But yeah, times were different then. I bet they got what was comin' to them, though." Maybelle picked up the bag and cleared the white circles. "Come on, we got to take this to her grave."

***

Reggie lay down on the couch, watching a football game he recorded the night before on his DVR. Today he was off work and enjoying the break. There had been no spooky occurrences last night, and he welcomed the reprieve. Tilting his Starbucks mug revealed it was empty. Getting up, he put on the kettle to make a fresh cup of coffee.

While the kettle boiled, Reggie went into the bathroom. As he unzipped his pants, an odd tapping sound made him turn his head.

He looked around, asking himself, "Where the hell is that coming from?" He stood on his toes to see if some kid was outside the window goofing about, but he couldn't see anything.

Tap, tap, tap, sounded again. Reggie now discerned where it was coming from. When he deduced its origins, realization rooted him to the spot.

Tap, tap, tap. Someone was tapping the glass...from inside the mirror. He knew instantly who and what it was. Trepidation flooded every part of his body. Reggie held onto the wall and counter. The room spun slowly at first and then picked up speed.

Stop! Get a grip. It's time I end this once and for all.

Flushing the toilet, he approached the mirror slowly, glancing around for some object to use as a weapon. Monica's hair straightener lay on the counter. Picking the device up, Reggie gripped it as he was now about to stare back at Lisa.

She folded her arms and glared at him with eyes full of contempt.

"Hey Reggie-kins. Miss me?" she said in a sing-song tone.

"Wha— what do you want?"

Lisa eyed what he held in his right hand. "Taking up hairdressing now?"

"Look, I'm sorry I left you behind, but I had no choice. They would've killed me if I didn't."

"And I'm supposed to forgive you for that? You left me to *die*."

"I went to get help and you know it! I loved you, Lis, can't you see that?"

"Loved me so much you abandoned me."

"I didn't abandon you," he shouted. "Didn't I just say—" Reggie stopped, sighing, putting down the straightener. He spoke again in a calm voice. "If you don't believe me, fine. I don't care. I'm sick of beating myself up all these years. I really loved you, but anyone else in my position would've done the same thing. I'm sorry you got shot. For a long time, I wished it were me instead of you. It's time to move on."

"Easy for you to say because you're still living, get to have a life, a relationship, everything I can't," Lisa retorted.

"What more do you want me to say or do?"

"Kill yourself and we can be together."

In a trice, it all made sense. This wasn't Lisa. The girl he knew would never ask him to do something like that. "Wha— what are you?"

"I'm Lisa. Remember?"

"She wouldn't ask me to do that, no matter how angry she was."

"Death can change a person."

"Not her. Not my Lis."

"Really?" Lisa giggled and lowered her head for a second. When she rose it again, her blue eyes were now glowing a bright red. "Ding, ding, ding." Her voice was now deeper and distorted. "Looks like we got a winner. Took you long enough, *lover-boy*."

"Oh God."

"He's not gonna be much use to you now." Demon Lisa walked closer to the mirror, her face less than an inch from the glass. Arching her head back, she head-butted the glass with all her might.

Reggie jumped, a spider-web-type crack now formed in the mirror.

Blood trickled down her forehead.

"What the hell?" he yelled.

Once more she hit the mirror full force with her forehead. The crack widened.

This time Lisa punched it, an imprint of her fist making the fissure wider. Soon, she was able to slip her fingers through to tear away the glass.

"Crap," Reggie screamed, turning around, twisting the door handle left and right, but the door wouldn't budge.

"Going somewhere?" the demon asked with a sneer, grunting as she continued to tear what shards remained so she could fit through.

"Open up," Reggie barked, shaking the door, almost ripping it off its hinges.

"You're mine now, *Reggie-kins*," Demon Lisa warned while putting her left leg and upper torso through. Blood dripped from her forehead wound.

"No!" he roared. "Get back." He hit her across the face with the straightener.

She fell back into the hole. Behind the girl was only an eerie black void of nothingness.

Seizing his opportunity, Reggie turned the handle on the door. It opened. Running out of the house, he stopped while outside for a moment, bent over, hands on knees.

Humming from the hallway made him turn around. Walking toward him was Demon Lisa, head wound still leaking blood, a sinister smirk on her face. "You're mine forever, Reggie-kins."

He began backing away, shaking his head. "Not a chance." Spinning on his heels, he dashed out onto the road.

A car screeched to a halt but not soon enough for Reggie to see it coming. The vehicle hit him hard. The impact launched him into the air, and he came back down with a sickening thud.

"Oh my God. Are you okay?" Reggie heard a man scream before he closed his eyes.

***

Maybelle parked her car outside the cemetery. She and Jared got out of it. Maybelle carried the can of pure salt containing the pocket watch.

"We're almost done, J. Another case nearly finished. Let's bring it home."

"For sure. I'm down with that. Do you think she's here?"

"Oh, I bet. She wants closure just as much as we do." Maybelle walked toward the rusty wrought-iron gate, pushing it open.

Jared followed her in and closed it. He surveyed rows of headstones, but Madame Farooq wasn't there. "I can't see her anywhere."

"Try and focus again."

"Hold up, why can't you see her? You're more powerful than me."

"She came to you first, so maybe she'll only appear when you call her."

"Okay. Never thought of that." Jared shut both eyes and centered himself, casting aside all thoughts again. Sounds of birds singing and cars passing by didn't distract him.

Down here, he heard her say in his mind.

Jared combed all the graves. On the far right, tucked away in an obscure corner, black mist swirled around before taking the form of a woman.

"I think I know where she's buried." This time Jared took the lead as they went to her grave.

Someone had carved "M. F. Farooq" onto a simple wooden cross and embedded it in the ground. Withered flowers were beneath the cross.

Madame Farooq stood there, hands clasped in front of her. A slow smile of relief spread across her face.

"Merci to you both. This means so much."

"What would you like us to do with the pocket watch?" Jared asked.

"Put it there," she replied, pointing to the grave

"But won't somebody steal it again?" Maybelle said.

"Not this time," Madame Farooq replied confidently.

Maybelle took the white bag out of the can of salt, emptying its contents just underneath the cross.

Raising her head and with both arms cast out, a white light cocooned the ghost's eyes.

The ground crumbled beneath where her father's pocket watch lay, swallowing it.

"Wow," Jared said, taking a step back, slowly shaking his head in disbelief.

Grass regenerated immediately, covering up where the hole was seconds ago.

Her eyes returned to normal. "Together at last. No one steal from Madame Farooq again."

"That's for damn sure. Now can you tell us what we can do to save Reggie and Zane?" Jared said.

"Oui. Take those." Two bright red roses appeared at Jared's feet. "Give one to each man. Tell him to take it to grave of person he hurt or killed. They must apologize to break spell."

"Wait a second, they could've done that all along?" Jared asked, his voice raised in displeasure.

"*Non*. The roses can break the spell I cast on Papa's watch." She cocked her right ear as if being told something by someone. She spun around, glancing at the horizon.

"What's wrong?" Maybelle asked.

"Hurry. Demon knows men are almost saved." She raised a hand to her mouth in horrified astonishment. "*Mon Dieu*, he'll kill them. Go. Now!"

"Thanks," Jared said, picking up both roses.

While running back to their cars, Maybelle asked, "Do you have your cell on you?"

"Yeah. Why?"

"I forgot mine. We need to ring Zane and tell him to get himself and Reggie to a church. If there's a demon after them, it can't touch 'em there."

Maybelle pressed a button on her keys to open the white 2011 Renault Clio.

"You got his number?" Jared asked.

Maybelle reached inside a back pocket in her jeans, taking out a scrap of paper. "Here." Jared took it. "Ride with me. You can come back and get your car later."

They sat into hers. Punching in Zane's number, Jared said, "I hope we're not too late."

***

Another four hours to go for the shift to be over, was all Zane could think about to get through the day. Part of him wished he could get a job somewhere else, but with most businesses closed down because of Covid, he was fortunate to have this one. Waiting tables was not his idea of earning money.

The worst part of working in a grocery store was stocking shelves. *Can't wait to get this over and done with.* Each box of cereal was put neatly on the shelf in a straight row. As Mr. Roberts often told him, they were to be lined like a military column with not one box out of place.

Just as Zane was about to put up another one, he paused. Sounds of an animal whimpering in the next aisle made the hairs on his neck stand on end.

Oh, God, please no! Zane took each step as if he were about to walk close to a cliff's edge, anticipating the worst. Sweat trickled down his back. Standing at the aisle's edge, he peeked around.

There, lying with two rib bones protruding through beige fur was Titus. Blood pooled around him, oozing from his wound and mouth. The dog howled and whined in pain. A large black tire mark streaked across Titus' body.

Zane snapped his head back as the animal stared in his direction as if sensing the man's presence. *Oh crap. What am I going to do?*

Like a fleeing thief, he inched along the aisle, one painstaking step at a time, being careful not to make a sound.

As he reached the other end, Titus walked into view, rib bones still protruding. A trail of blood was behind him. Saliva dripped from his incisors as he began to growl. With his eyes narrowed, Titus walked toward Zane.

"Look, I'm sorry, all right. I never meant for you to get hurt," Zane said.

Titus barked three times and quickened his pace.

Passing the checkout counter, Zane darted for the front exit. Titus was behind him. He could hear the animal gaining with its barking coming closer.

While still running, he fumbled for his keys. Zane pressed a button to unlock the car. Getting in, he slammed the door. The roaring engine drowned out the barking of Titus outside. Reversing out of the parking lot, Zane drove home, leaving Titus in a cloud of dust, but he wondered for how long.

Fifteen minutes later, Zane was home, barricading himself inside his bedroom, pushing the bed against the door. Sitting in a corner hugging both knees, he began praying.

"Please, God, please protect me. If you get me out of this, I swear I'll go back to church. *I swear*! Pleas—"

His praying came to an abrupt halt when howling reverberated around the hall.

"Damn!" he cried.

Titus' growling drew closer with each second until it was finally outside the bedroom door.

Taking out his cell, Zane dialed Reggie's number. It continued ringing until the busy tone kicked in.

"Come on, Reg, pick up!" He tried again but there was no answer. "Crap." He was about to dial Maybelle's number but a call came from one he didn't recognize. Zane pressed the answer button.

"Hello?"

"This is Jared. I need you to listen, all right?"

"Ar—are you guys done yet?" Zane's voice trembled.

"Whoa, what's wrong?" Jared asked.

"It's here, at my house again. It's trying to kill me."

"Dang." Jared told Maybelle what Zane said. She said something he couldn't quite hear. "My aunt says can you get to your car?"

"I'll try but—"

Zane fell silent when an invisible force pushed the bed back from his door. It scraped along the floor.

"You there?" he heard Jared yell.

Zane stood up, opening the window to make his escape. "Yes. I might be able to get to it."

"Is there a church near you?" Jared said.

"St. Peter's. About two blocks away."

"Go there and stay inside. Can you get Reggie to go there, too?"

"Tried calling but couldn't get through to him."

"Damn, hope he's okay. Call out his number." Zane told Jared the man's number. "Cool. I'll try and ring him. We'll meet you at St. Peter's in about ten minutes."

Suddenly, something propelled the bed, pinning Zane against the wall. The cell fell from his hand. He could hear Jared screaming something on the other end.

Titus sauntered in. Licking his lips, he continued to advance like a tiger ready to devour its prey.

Zane tried to push the bed away from him but it wouldn't budge, only pressing tighter against his stomach.

Titus looked to his right. Zane jumped as the bed moved toward the window, blocking his exit. Terror filled his face. An empty space was all that stood between him and Titus.

The dog's eyes came alive with a red glow. Its rib bones that stuck out were now tucked inside, the wound sealing itself shut.

In the man's peripheral vision, he saw a knife on the locker beside him. He had used it the night before to peel an apple while watching TV.

What good will that do? He's dead. Zane grabbed it anyway, hoping that the weapon might slow down his dead tormentor.

Titus' attention switched to the knife.

Something grabbed the man's hand, forcing it to the wall. He tried with all his strength to resist Titus' power, but its grip was too strong. Now Titus tried to pry open Zane's fingers, starting with the thumb, wrestling the weapon from his grasp.

"Stop it. Please, leave me alone!"

Not...until...you're mine, a deep malevolent voice shot back telepathically.

"No," Zane yelled. Instantly, whatever held his hand released its hold just as Titus lunged at him. Zane raised the knife, thrusting it into the dead animal's stomach just as the dog was an inch from his face. A loud yelp confirmed contact. The red glow around its eyes faded. Now he lay lifeless on the floor.

"Holy sh—" Zane's jaw trembled, staring on in disbelief at what was before him.

Quickly snapping into action, he forced back the window farther. Climbing up on the bed, he put one leg over the headboard.

Whimpering and a sloshing sound from behind him almost made Zane leap. With a quick glance over his shoulder, he saw the knife was being ejected out of Titus' stomach.

Zane threw the other leg over the headboard and dashed to the car.

Switching on the ignition, he cursed when Titus now bounded out of the bedroom window. Slamming his foot on the accelerator, Zane started for St. Peter's.

***

As Reggie opened his eyes, he heard a voice say, "He's coming around." Pain in his right leg and hip greeted him, both feeling loose and wobbly, like Jell-O. They had strapped Reggie onto a gurney.

Two men were near him, one on either side. They wore white and red windbreakers. Both were EMTs he guessed as sirens wailed. The man on his left was the older of the two.

"Oh, my leg," Reggie moaned, trying to sit up.

"Take it easy, buddy," the older EMT said, putting a hand to Reggie's chest, forcing him to be still. "My name's Dave and this is Jonas. You've been hurt pretty bad."

"You're on your way to the hospital. Just relax," Jonas added.

"Need to..." Reggie found it difficult to finish the sentence, excruciating pain disturbed his train of thought. He kept clenching his fist to deal with the agony he felt. Shock numbed some of it.

"What's that?" Dave said, lifting the oxygen mask

"Contact…Monica."

"Is that your girlfriend?" Jonas asked. Reggie nodded.

"Not for much longer," Demon Lisa interjected.

Reggie raised his head, he saw her with a ravenous grin sitting below Dave. "Don't worry, Reggie-kins," Her blue eyes reverted to burning red. Demon Lisa's sweet, innocent voice changed to a deep, sinister tone. "This won't hurt a bit." She stood up and walked through Dave.

"No, no. Keep...away!"

Dave put the oxygen mask back on him. "He's going into shock." Pinning Reggie's shoulders, he continued. "Take it easy, sir. Relax. You're safe now."

"You're really not," Demon Lisa taunted, her hand reaching through the oxygen mask, covering the mouth and just underneath his nose, cutting off all supply of air.

Reggie shook his head, wriggling to break free. He moved left and right, restricted by the straps.

"Ease your pain, just let go. You've lived with the guilt for too long. Let me take it away," she said, feigning sympathy.

"No..." Trying with all his might to escape her deathly white hand, he moved his head about with the constant image of Monica in his mind. *Got to...stay alive...for her.* The thought of never seeing her again made him fight more. No more dinners in front of the TV, Sunday afternoons spent laying under the shade of a tree, or the wonderful sex both enjoyed. These thoughts fueled his attempts further, moving his head about, trying to slip loose from the girl's hand.

The demon's grip proved difficult to elude as it seemed to grow abnormally, spreading out, covering the man's entire face. Now she was cutting off more oxygen with every passing second.

Soon, Reggie's eyes bulged, darkness creeping in from the sides. His lips began turning blue.

"Looks like he's in respiratory arrest," Dave said, ripping open Reggie's shirt and applying some oil to his chest. Next, he took out the defibrillator. "Clear!"

Reggie felt a shock run through him but it didn't stop the calmness he felt, surrendering more and more to it, no longer jerking or wriggling.

"I'm going again. Clear!" Dave pressed the defibrillator on Reggie's chest.

Another shockwave flooded his body but it didn't stop the total serenity enveloping him.

"ETA to hospital?" Jonas shouted out to the driver.

"Five minutes," was the answer.

"I'll try one last time," Dave announced. "Clear."

Another wave of electricity went through Reggie but now he had surrendered fully, no longer offering any resistance.

Demon Lisa crouched beside him, her mouth right next to his left ear, "That's it. Don't fight it. Give in to me."

Goodbye...Monica... A single tear rolled down his cheek as the last spark of life left his eyes.

***

Zane turned off the engine as he parked the car opposite St. Peter's. Throughout the journey there, he kept checking his rear-view mirror, expecting Titus to jump out at any second. With a quick scan of the side mirrors, Zane got out and locked the door. He stared at the steps leading up to the double wooden doors of the church.

Just as he was about to put his foot on the first step, barking from behind made him halt for a second. He knew it all too well now.

Titus' barking now turned to growling. The dog was standing beside Zane's car. Titus ran toward him.

Zane fled up the steps.

Suddenly, he fell to the ground, howling in agony as large teeth sank into his leg.

Did you really think you could escape ME? the demon's voice boomed in Zane's head.

"Oh, God. I said sorry already, okay? Don't kill me," Zane yelled.

You mortals think everything can be solved by saying 'sorry'.

Zane screamed when bones cracked in his shin as Titus continued to sink his teeth further.

He tried through teary eyes to kick Titus away, but it had little effect, with the dead animal keeping its tight hold for another minute until letting go on its own.

Zane tried to crawl away, but the pain was too much for him to even move. It required too much energy and it sapped his strength.

Titus continued to taunt Zane as he began circling him. *All mortals are pathetic and weak. The stench of guilt is repulsive...just like you. If only you could experience the pain Old Man Hammond felt when he found Titus, left to die on the road.*

Tears continued to stream down his cheeks, and his heart pounded as he stammered, "It w—was an a—accident."

Titus paused as he stood beside Zane. He tried to move further away, but Titus jumped on him. *Don't worry, weakling.* Baring his teeth, he continued, *I'll end all the pain by taking your miserable life.*

"No!"

Titus' eyes flared a fiery red glow. Saliva dripped off his teeth as he opened his mouth for the kill.

Just as the dog was about to rip open Zane's throat, a car screeched to a halt in front of the church.

Jared and Maybelle got out with the woman holding a can of something in her hands. Opening its lid, she sprinkled what looked like salt on the dog. Once the salt hit him, it sizzled on his skin like hot oil in a frying pan.

Titus whimpered, jumping off Zane, retreating.

"Oh, man, that's nasty," Jared muttered with a quick glance at Zane's leg.

"Help me!" the man screamed, blood running down his ankle.

"Start saying the Archangel Michael Prayer, Jared," Maybelle said while throwing more salt at Titus.

Jared sprinkled some water on the entity while reciting the prayer.

Titus backed off some more.

"That's it, keep dousing him with the holy water, J!" Maybelle put down the can of salt and helped Zane up.

"Ow!" He grimaced, blood oozing out from the puncture marks. "Can't stand on it."

"It's okay, I got you." Maybelle put his left arm around her shoulder.

Zane hobbled to the car. "Your seat's gonna be all bloody," he said.

"Let me worry about that. Come on."

Maybelle helped him into the back of her car. When he sat in, she gave him a crucifix.

"What's this going to do?" He eyed it in confusion while trying to remain calm despite the pain soaring up and down his leg.

"That will protect you." Maybelle opened the trunk, taking out a bandage. Gingerly, she wrapped it around his leg, with him wincing, roaring when the material touched the deep wounds.

Through the front windshield, in the distance he could see Jared douse holy water on the dog until it ran away a few minutes later, disappearing after turning a corner up ahead.

Running back to the car, he sat in. "I think that thing's gone."

"Yeah, but for how long?" Maybelle replied, now behind the wheel, having finished bandaging Zane's shin.

When Jared clicked his seatbelt in place, she took off to the hospital.

PART FOUR: FAREWELL OLD FRIEND

A week later, Zane wheeled himself into the graveyard. The demon who bit into Zane's leg broke the tibia and fibula. Maybelle gave him the crucifix, instructing doctors to keep it at his bedside.

The next day after the surgery, she told him about the ritual that had to be done of placing a rose she'd give him at Old Man Hammond's grave.

Four days later, the hospital discharged him. Zane's mother took him to their house. He kept the crucifix at his side as much as possible. That night, it was only when he'd eaten and was comfortable that he was told by his mother about Reggie's passing. At first he didn't believe it. Reggie was a young man with so much living to do. Soon he realized that the same demon must have attacked his friend before coming to him. Zane missed the funeral but Monica promised to take him to see the grave in a few days.

That night, as he lay in bed staring at the ceiling, all the happy times he had spent with his friend began coming back. The laughs they shared while playing fighting games online or in the arcade, and all the times they used to ride their bikes around the neighborhood. Even just the simplest thing of texting Reggie when he felt down or worried, something he could never do again

The following morning, Monica wheeled him into the cemetery. A bouquet lay on his lap. When they stopped at Reggie's grave, she stood beside Zane, sobbing while holding his hand.

"I wish it had been me instead—"

"Don't," Monica interrupted him. "He wouldn't want that."

"I feel this is all my fault."

"I didn't bring you here so you would beat yourself up," Monica said in a gentle but resolved tone. "This is your chance to say goodbye. So I'm going to leave you alone for a minute. I'll be by the gate." Monica let go of his hand. Stones crunched under her feet as she walked away.

"What can I say, Reg? I messed up big time." Zane's voice broke and his eyes welled up. "If only I hadn't bought that damn watch, we'd still be hanging together. I'm so sorry. I'm so—" Zane couldn't speak anymore as he cried inconsolably. Burying his face into both hands, his shoulders shook as tears snuck out between each finger.

Monica came to his side again and hugged him.

He continued to mourn loudly for the closest friend he ever had, with his head on her chest. Drying his eyes, Zane placed the bouquet of flowers on Reggie's grave.

"See you, buddy. I'll be back again soon." He nodded to Monica that it was time to leave. She blew a kiss at the grave before Zane wheeled himself out of the cemetery.

***

Jared sat alone in Jackie's Diner with only a half-empty mug of hot chocolate to keep him company. The news of Reggie Danes' death shook him to the core. He tried ringing him before they rescued Zane but couldn't reach him. For two nights straight he failed to get some sleep. In his mind he could still see the tear-streaked face of Monica, staring forlornly into the grave as Reggie's coffin was being lowered. The 'if onlys' ran through his mind.

If only we had gotten to him sooner, he'd still be alive.

If only we'd known about the demon being in two places at the same time we could've let Reggie know and saved him.

Jared's stomach churned at the mental images of Reggie's horrific injuries, shuddering at the thought of the pain he must have felt. Along with the absolute fear facing the entity while being strapped to a gurney inside an ambulance. Jared learned about what happened when he overheard a couple talking about it at the funeral. One of them knew the EMTs and he told them about what Reggie said before dying.

Poor guy. Never stood a chance.

"I hope that ain't a cup of 'beat-yourself-up' juice you're drinking." Maybelle's voice disturbed his thinking.

"You following me around now, Aunt Belle?" he said with a wry half grin.

"No. I phoned your house and your mom said you were here. Can I join?"

"Sure."

Maybelle sat down on the opposite side of the booth. "So let me guess, you're angry over Reggie's death, right?"

"Damn straight. Aren't you?"

"Of course, but you can't save everyone every time, J. That's something you got to learn. We did the best we could."

"I know but..." His voice trailed off, his brown eyes never leaving the table.

"Look, I know it sucks, a young man and his life snuffed out like that. It's wrong, but we saved Zane. If we weren't there, he'd be dead, too."

"Yeah, still though. I just wish we could've rescued him. How can we do what we do if somebody's gonna die? Why can't God protect them?"

"Sometimes in life, J, you can't save everyone, no matter how much we want to." Maybelle held his hand. "It killed me inside too watching his folks and girlfriend burying him, knowing they'd never see him again. Don't think I ain't feeling nothing."

"I didn't say that, Belle. I know you're hurting but..." Jared's voice broke.

"Now listen here, Jared Anthony Duval. Don't you dare go blaming yourself for what happened. We did the best we could. In our line of work, sometimes you win, sometimes you lose. We take the Ws when we can."

"Even if someone else dies?"

"Yes, even that. I may sound like a broken record, but because of what we do, Mrs. Miller still gets to have her son instead of burying him. The demon didn't fully win."

"Instead he got half of one."

"So did we, J! You gotta be like that cup of hot chocolate. You gotta look at life from a glass-half-full point of view. I know it stinks he's dead but don'tcha think Reggie is glad we saved Zane?"

"Yeah...yeah, guess so."

"Of course he is. This is your calling. Like every job, there'll be good days and bad. The thing is, never stop what you're doing. We *do* make a difference." Maybelle cleared another tear from his smooth face.

He offered a better but still weak attempt at a smile in return.

"Guess you're right, Belle. Thanks."

"I know I'm right."

"You ever lost someone before?"

"Twice. It doesn't get easier but like my mama once told me, 'In every game, there's gotta be a loser sometime'. Meaning we can't win them all but the thing is, we win a lot more than we lose. Always remember that, too."

Jared squeezed Maybelle's hand in appreciation. "Thanks Belle. Sure am glad to have you here with me."

"Wouldn't have it any other way." Maybelle gave a quick glance at Jared's still-steaming cup of chocolate. "So, you gonna buy your aunt a drink before we pick up Zane?"

"I suppose your help don't come cheap, huh?"

"Hey, if I were an NFL player, no team could afford me."

Jared laughed and Maybelle joined in. "They sure couldn't. The usual?"

"Uh-huh," she said while nodding.

"Coming up."

***

Twenty-four hours later Zane was back, but this time at Old Man Hammond's grave with Jared and Maybelle in tow. As he wheeled himself down, in a bag hanging on one of the wheelchair handles was Madame Farooq's rose. It was Zane's first time at the former neighbor's final resting place. All along he felt too guilty to come here. Now his life depended on it.

He turned the chair to face the grave.

"Do you want to be alone?" Maybelle asked.

"No. It's okay. What do I do? Just say sorry and put the rose on it?"

"Basically, yeah," she replied.

"All right." He wheeled himself in a little closer. "I'm probably the last person you expected to see, Mr. Hammond. Guess by now you know what I did. I never meant for Titus to get killed like that. I know 'sorry' doesn't bring him back but I've come to make my peace." He picked up the flower. "Just hope you can forgive me because I'm really sorry." An image of Reggie in happier times flashed through his mind. His breath became shaky while continuing. "It has cost me too much so I know your pain." Zane placed the flower next to a small ceramic statue of a cherub.

A gentle, warm breeze caressed his cheek. Calmness came over him. The heavy burden of guilt that had been on his shoulders for many years now evaporated. Inside he felt a certain lightness. Zane's heart swelled with joy.

"I think it worked," he announced, smiling.

"I think it did too," Maybelle said.

"So does that mean the demon's gone?" Zane asked.

"Guess it does. We did everything the lady told us to," Maybelle replied.

"I'm sorry about your friend. I know you two were tight," Jared added.

Bowing his head in momentary shame, Zane said, "Not as sorry as me."

Maybelle squeezed his shoulder in comfort. "You can't blame yourself. Nobody knew that pocket-watch was cursed."

"I know but it still don't make things better." Zane cleared his throat, stifling a tear. "Thanks for doing all this. I appreciate it. If it's okay, can we go? I've had my fill of this place over the last two days."

"Sure. We'll take you home." Maybelle and Jared followed Zane as he wheeled himself toward her car.

***

Jared and his aunt waved goodbye to Zane and his family as she drove away.

"Do you really think everything's gonna be okay now?" Jared asked.

"I think he's gonna be safe. Did you feel something when he apologised?"

"Kinda. Not too sure. I just felt something warm around us."

“That was the curse being lifted. He’ll be fine.” Silence fell on them for a moment until Maybelle broke it again. “How about you? You gonna be okay?”

“Huh?” Jared raised his eyebrows in confusion.

“I get that this is still kind of scary, helping ghosts cross over, fighting demons an’ all.”

“Damn straight. Sure ain’t no walk in the park.”

“That, it’s not. Like I said before, this is your destiny.”

“I know...still kind of frightens me, though.” Then a thought struck him. “One thing I can’t understand.”

“What’s that?”

“How come Madame Farooq appeared to me? I mean, there’s gotta be other psychics here in Hopps Town, so why me?”

“To ghosts, psychics are like radios: they tune into the energy they like. If the spirit feels they can work with a certain person, they will. So Madame Farooq obviously liked you.”

Another thought occurred to Jared. “One other thing. Stevenson. What about him? How come he wasn’t affected?”

“Maybe it’s because he had no guilt or did anything wrong in the past. Demons feed off of it. So that’s why he wasn’t attacked like Zane or Reggie.”

“Why didn’t Madame Farooq just tell me about the pocket watch at the start?”

“Whoa, good thing it was only one last question. It could be part of you developing your gift even more. Who knows? You gotta admit, though, it’s cool riding shotgun with me, solving cases like Dean and Sam Winchester.”

“Yeah, it’s cool. I’m Dean, though.”

“Pfft. You wish, homeboy,” Maybelle scoffed. They shared a brief laugh.

Once they stopped, Maybelle studied him before continuing. “When I first started doing all this, it used to scare the crap outta me not knowing what was gonna appear. Is that what scares you, too? Not knowing who’s gonna come?”

“Uh-huh, sort of.”

“Don’t be ashamed of that. Everyone gets afraid now and again, J.

But call on your guardian angel for help too. That's what they're there for, to protect you."

"Yeah, I know..." Jared replied, his tone not too convincing.

"Is that doubt I hear?"

"No…I don't know...maybe."

"Put that out of your mind now, J. They're there for protection."

Jared stared at his hands for a moment, twiddling his thumbs before putting on the radio to change the subject.

Maybelle turned it off. "Hey, don't turn on that when I'm talkin' to you! I'm giving you good advice."

Jared lowered his head in embarrassment. "Not that I don't appreciate it and all...but I hate talking about angels and stuff."

Maybelle shot him a quick understanding smile. "I know it's not 'manly' to express your feelings but you can tell me anything, anytime. Understood?"

"Got it."

"Just wanna say one last thing. See what happened to Zane?" Jared nodded. "Let that be a lesson to you. Sins from the past always come back to haunt you. Don't do wrong to nobody because karma...well, you know what they call that."

"The B word?"

"Uh-huh. *Now* you can turn on the radio."

Jared pressed the on button, cycling through the stations until he came to one playing R&B songs.

Maybelle began tapping the steering wheel, bopping her head, moving her shoulders to the music's beat. "Show Aunt Maybelle some of your moves."

Jared put a hand up, hiding his face in mortification.

"Don't get all shy on me now, mister. Come on, loosen up."

"Oh God," Jared said, sinking further into his seat.

Maybelle laughed as she continued to bop and move to the music.

***

Jessica sat at the diner table looking at her phone while waiting for her mom. In front of her was a cappuccino and a delicious hot chocolate with marshmallows bobbing on top of some cream. "Body Found in Construction Site" screamed the headline on the front page of a folded newspaper at their table.

A year ago, she would never have thought having lunch with her mom was possible because of their toxic relationship. Even though what happened at the well would always haunt everyone involved, she was kind of glad things unfolded the way they did. After the exorcism, Jessica found the inner strength to confront Bertha, to tell her what she'd been feeling for a long time. This transformed Bertha from a mean, sometimes violent alcoholic to the loving mom she had been before Jessica's dad left eight years ago. Now she could feel at ease around her and talk to her like a daughter's supposed to.

"Hey there, honeybun," Bertha said.

Jessica slid the phone into her pocket. "Hi. Didn't see you there. Got the hot chocolate you wanted."

Bertha placed her handbag by the wall before sitting down. She took a sip, her lips curling to form a smile of approval. "Mmm, that's good. So, are you all set to go back to college tomorrow?"

"Almost. Just got one more bag to pack so..." Jessica sighed, not wanting to leave Hopps Town. Her break away from college had been fun. She and Bertha had painted each other's nails and stayed up late some nights watching movies while sharing a bowl of popcorn. Once the lockdown restrictions were lifted, they visited the spa and had a movie night. Jessica heard for the first time all these wonderful stories about her great granddad, how he showed Bertha how to bait a hook to catch fish, and how to slow down and spend some evenings watching dusk creep in at the backdrop of an orange horizon. Jessica had seen a side to her mom that she never knew existed.

"I'm sure gonna miss you. We had a real swell time, didn't we?" Bertha remarked.

"Sure did. Can't wait for Spring Break and we can do some more stuff."

"Looking forward to it already." Taking a teaspoon, Bertha ate some marshmallows.

Jessica laughed as a small bit of cream lodged on the tip of her mother's nose.

"What's so funny?" Bertha asked.

Pointing to her own nose, Jessica replied, "You got some there."

Taking a tissue, Bertha let slip a gentle chuckle while wiping the cream off. "They really have the best hot chocolate in town. So, got all your assignments done?"

"Yup. Printed them off yesterday and read through them last night."

"I bet it was exciting reading, huh?" Bertha quipped with a half-smile.

"Oh, riveting." Jessica took a sip of her own cappuccino.

With a pensive expression, Bertha stirred her drink.

Jessica knew her mother wanted to say something but opening up was still hard for her to do. "What is it, Mom?"

"I'm so proud of you, Jess. You're this young, beautiful, amazing daughter and you're so driven despite everything...that I put you through. One of the twelve steps is that we've got to make amends with all the people we hurt and..." Bertha's voice broke, putting on one of those famous poker faces but not wholly hiding guilt and regret. "How can you still love me after all that I did? I was," Her voice trembled, eyes welled up. "I was the mother from hell and still you wanna spend time with me." Bertha shielded her face from others in the diner.

Jessica took Bertha's left hand in her own. "I love you because you're my mom. Yeah, you were mean to me for a while but you always made sure we had food on the table and a roof over our heads. You're now the mom I wanted since Dad left."

Bertha surrendered, no longer fighting back the tears. She cried and Jessica hugged her, aware that lots of eyes were now falling on them.

After Bertha's crying stopped, she wiped away tears from her cheeks. "I really don't deserve you but thank God you're mine."

"I'm proud of you," Jessica said, still holding her mom's hand. "Everything that's happened over the last year, all the changes that were made, the work promotions, *you* made that happen. Nobody else."

"Stop or I'll start crying again." Bertha fanned her face with both hands, taking deep breaths. "I couldn't have done it all without you, Jess. Love you, baby." Bertha squeezed her hand in gratitude.

Jessica drank some more of her cappuccino. They chatted for another twenty minutes before Bertha's lunch break was over.

***

Zane sat outside the café, waiting for his espresso to arrive. His mother had to do some grocery shopping and he just wanted to sit there while she was gone. She'd pick him up on the way back. It was his first time being on his own outside of the house. The blue skies and sunshine were a big contrast to the gloom he felt inside of him.

"Here you go, sir," the beaming server said, placing the espresso in front of him. There was a complimentary cookie on the side of the plate. "Can I get you anything else?"

"No, that's fine, thanks," Zane replied, and she left.

He scanned the crowds passing by, half expecting to see Reggie walking amongst them, getting a coffee or soda from Roberts's store. *Just can't believe he's gone. It's not right. How can this happen? How come I survived and he didn't?*

He gripped the table to control his anger, taking deep breaths, exhaling them slowly.

"Fancy seeing you here, stranger," a sweet voice said, stopping him from sinking further into a pit of despair. It was Monica, wearing dark sunshades. He knew that this was to hide the red around her eyes from crying.

"Just needed to get out, to clear my head." Zane attempted a friendly grin but knew deep down that he failed miserably.

Now it was Monica's turn to feign one of her own. "I know what you mean. It's been…hard for me, too. Can I join you?"

"Sure."

Monica pulled up a chair and put her handbag down beside it. There had been a little drizzle of rain earlier that morning so she wiped the seat dry before sitting down. "How have you been sleeping?"

"Lucky if I can get a few hours in. You?"

"Me too. I'm thinking of moving into a new apartment across town. It's not the same…" Monica put a hand up to her mouth as her voice choked with emotion.

Zane hoped that a flood of tears wouldn't follow.

She cleared her throat before continuing. "Sorry."

"No need to apologize. Sitting here seeing these people walking around and not seeing him. I keep expecting his texts or phone calls every day."

"I know. Every morning I turn over and expect to see him there beside me…and he's not."

"Should've been me, Monica. It should've been—"

"I'm gonna have to stop you there. I didn't come here to make you feel bad or to hear you beat yourself up. Like I said at the grave, he wouldn't want that. Reggie loved you like a brother."

"I…I…" Zane couldn't get the words out and gripped the table tight to prevent himself from breaking out in tears.

Monica reached over, squeezing his left hand. "Let it all out. Don't hide it just cos I'm here."

"I miss him so much!" Zane could not withhold his emotions any longer as he bawled. Monica continued to rub his arm. Right now, he didn't care if people stared at him as he cried.

Monica sobbed too.

"Are you all right, guys?" a red-haired petite server asked, creases forming on her forehead in concern.

Zane wiped his cheeks, cleared his throat, and took a deep breath before he answered her. "Yeah, we're fine. We just lost somebody close to us, that's all."

"Oh, I'm so sorry." He didn't look at the girl as she spoke but he could hear the awkwardness in her tone. She left almost immediately.

"Sorry. I feel like a jackass for being like this," Zane said to Monica, continuing to wipe tears from his face.

"Don't, that's all part of the healing process."

"Reggie was lucky to have a girl like you."

"He had a great friend in you, too."

"Thanks."

"But you gotta remember this. You got a second chance in life. Think of it as a clean slate. It's time to do whatever you want to. I'm sure Reggie would want you to move forward."

Zane thought about her words for a moment, concluding that she was right. "Yeah, guess this is like a second chance. Never thought of that before."

"There you go. And you know what?" He remained silent, waiting for her to continue. "We should meet every week like this to catch up."

"Sounds good to me."

"Cool." Monica stood up. "Same time and place next week?"

"You bet."

"Great. See you then." She bent down and kissed his left cheek, whispering, "Hang in there." Monica patted his shoulder before leaving.

Zane took a sip of his cappuccino, the woman's words still ringing in his ears. *She's right, it's time for me to become a better person. I owe that to Reg.*

A woman in a tattered, camel-colored trench coat dragging a heavy suitcase came toward him as she made her way up the street. He recognized her; it was the vagrant he had seen outside the store before rescuing Billy from the bullies.

And I know just where to start. "Excuse me, ma'am?"

The vagrant stopped, squinting her eyes to see him because of the strong sunlight. "You talkin' to me, mista?"

"Yeah. Here," Zane took out a ten-dollar bill from his pocket, handing the note to her, "buy yourself some food or a coffee on me."

"Gee…uh, thank you, sir." The old woman took the money, nodding her head in appreciation. Stuffing it into one of the pockets in the tattered coat, she walked on.

I swear, Reg, I'm gonna chase those dreams we often talked about and make you proud of me.

Zane took another sip of the hot drink, his heart swelling with joy, a renewed vigor coursing through his veins. *I won't let you down, buddy.*

***

Jessica washed her face in the bathroom. In the background, she had YouTube music videos playing on the phone which was propped up on a shelf. After lunch with her mother, she had spent the last hour packing her bags and giving the school assignments another once over.

While drying her face, the phone rang. It was Jared.

"Hey." She put him on speakerphone.

"Hi, Jess. What's up? You looking forward to going back to college?"

"Do I really need to answer that?"

"Nah, I'm just kidding," he laughed. "Did you have a good time?"

"Everything was great, actually. When do you head back?"

"Tomorrow too. Kind of sucks. Let's just hope it's worth it in the end."

"Sure. You see Adrian lately? I didn't get a chance to catch up with him."

"He's cool. I met him about a week ago. Long story."

Jessica's brows narrowed. "Are you guys okay? Did something happen?"

"Me and Adrian are fine. Just something else went on. I'll tell you another time. Just wanted to ring and see if everything went okay."

"No, all's good here. We definitely have to catch up during Spring Break."

"Damn straight. I gotta go. Got some stuff to do for tomorrow. Talk later, girl. Don't be afraid to shoot me a text sometime."

"Likewise. Talk later, Jared. Thanks for the call. Bye." Jessica pressed the end call button. She regretted not having the time to meet up with him, but it seemed like he was pretty busy. As for Adrian, he had only been around for less than a week, spending most of his time with Tina. She saw him with her a few times. He waved in Jessica's direction but didn't really talk to her. Part of Jessica envied Adrian being in a relationship, but she knew that focusing on school was what she needed to do right now. The degree in business law would allow her to get a well-paid job and be able to look after Bertha in the future.

Changing into her pajamas, Jessica climbed into bed. After an hour of reading, she fell asleep.

Jessica put the bag on the ground as she and her mom stood in the line of people waiting to get on the bus.

"You got everything, hon?" Bertha asked.

"Yup. Ready to go." Jessica stared down at her feet for a few seconds as an awkward moment hung between them.

Bertha broke the silence. "So will you get to the campus at around eight?"

"Hopefully yeah."

"Okay, sweetie. Well, I guess I better go. Have to get back to the store before my break's over." She gave Jessica a tight hug. "So proud of you."

"I know, Mom." She patted her mother's back twice.

Breaking the embrace, Bertha wiped a tear from her eye. "Gonna miss ya when you're gone."

"Me too. I'll call later tonight when I get in."

A tall, middle-aged man wearing a white shirt and black trousers walked halfway up the row of people and announced, "Bus leaves in twenty minutes, folks. Get your tickets ready."

"Guess that's my cue to go. Bye, Jess. Talk to you tonight." Bertha blew her a kiss as she walked away.

Fifteen minutes later, Jessica put her bag in the luggage compartment. She showed the ticket to the bus driver who stamped it.

Suddenly as she turned around to find a seat, Jessica now stood in a hallway. All the lights were out. Pictures that hung on the wall looked familiar. She realized this was home.

"What am I doing here? What's going on?"

Sobbing coming from Bertha's room piqued her curiosity. Jessica opened the door expecting to find her mom crying but she was lying on her side, sound asleep.

A girl stepping out from behind the curtains, almost made Jessica recoil.

"Who are you? How did you get in here and what do you want?" Jessica asked.

The intruder was the same height but in her early twenties. The girl's hair was dripping wet. There was something in her right hand. When she brought it up, Jessica gasped. It was a carving knife.

"Mom, wake up. Wake up!" Shaking Bertha vigorously didn't work. The woman was comatose. "Please leave. Don't hurt us," Jessica pleaded.

"Everyone has secrets, even her." The girl walked closer to Bertha. "Difference is, some are worse than others. And Mommy there, she got the worst of all."

"I don't know what you're talking about. Go or I'll call the cops."

"She does. I'll go when I get justice. And if not," The intruder's face contorted in a fuming rage, "then revenge." She lunged at Bertha, bringing the knife down hard.

"No!" Jessica screamed while sitting up. With a hand to her chest, she caught her breath. It took a moment to realize that she was in her bedroom back home. The dream was so real. Every detail was perfectly recreated.

"Who was that girl? What was all that about?" Sliding both feet into her slippers, Jessica went to the bathroom. Pulling back her red hair, she splashed some water onto her freckled face. She stood at the sink, taking a minute to compose herself, letting water drip off her nose and chin.

Closing both eyes, Jessica dried the water off.

After turning off the bathroom light, she froze.

There, embedded in the pillow, was the knife the girl had held in her dream. An icy chill now soared up her spine.

A clear message had been sent. Someone or something was out to get her and Bertha. Who or what it might be was uncertain right now, but one thing was for sure: she knew someone who could help find the answers.

The following is the start of the first chapter in, Dark Secrets - Book Three of, *The Hopps Town Series.*

August 2012

Mist swirled around where an injured woman lay. The blood flowing from her nose and mouth mingled with her long, silky black hair. Beams from her headlights, and those of another car, lit up the night sky. The running of the other car's engine drowned out the sound of crickets.

After being hit, taking each breath became harder. She had been standing beside her own vehicle when the other driver ploughed into her. She rolled onto the hood and up over the roof, falling back onto the ground with a force like a wrecking ball smashing into her petite body. She immediately felt a few ribs crack and her right leg fracture, and now a great weight rested on her chest, almost as if someone was sitting on it.

A woman was screaming from the other car.

"Oh my God. What did we do? Oh, Lord, there's a girl ... over there. I think we—"

"I ... ca—can't ... die," the injured woman said, her words slurring. "I ... got ... a ... child ..." The darkness of unconsciousness crept in from both sides of her vision. Keeping her eyes open was becoming even more of a chore: her lids grew heavier with each passing second, almost as heavy as the increasing weight on her upper body.

Love you, Anna, was the last thought she had before slipping away.

***

Present Day—Deep in the bowels of Hell

Harrowing cries surrounded Malik, along with rivers of fire snaking their way down pre-determined paths. Corrupt politicians were impaled on poles rammed up through their anuses and emerging out their skulls. Horned, winged demons stuffed the politicians' mouths with large fistfuls of dollar bills, and the souls' shouts of agonizing pain added to the already unbearable din of pleas for mercy swirling around Hell.

Bruised and wounded from the lashings he'd received, Malik shuffled along, both his feet and hands shackled. On either side of him stood tall, hulking, oil-black-skinned guards wearing Spartan leather skirts and swords sheathed in brown scabbards. They were fearsome creatures, a sort of wolf and gargoyle hybrid. Malik had the same form but with a thinner frame. They shoved him while continuing on. Heat from the rivers made Malik sweat profusely.

As the bound demon gazed at the wooden bridge that had to be crossed, he moaned, knowing that there were at least another twenty minutes of agony before they reached Satan's throne.

To Malik's far left was a high, ragged cliff. Many mortals were being prodded by the guards' spears, made to jump off into lakes of fire. Their skeletons floated past him, pieces of flesh still clinging to some of the skulls.

Hopefully that won't be me being thrown off the cliff, he thought, each step causing further pain.

Soon they arrived. One guard placed a large hand on Malik's shoulder, forcing him to kneel.

On his throne of bones, Satan sat staring down at him.

Malik dared not look up—not only out of respect and shame, but also due to Satan's hideous appearance. The fallen angel was twelve feet tall, with red-raw skin and a horn looming large on either side of his head. His flaming yellow eyes could penetrate deep into the most hardened soul.

"We meet once more, Malik," Satan boomed.

"Ye—Yes, my lord." Malik's eyes stayed focused on the ground. It pulsed like a human heart.

"You failed me, *again*. That human was supposed to kill those children, and you *failed*!"

"Everything was going well, my lord, until ..." Malik shuddered at the thought of saying Jesus' name. "He intervened."

"Excuses. That's all I hear lately: excuses." Satan banged his humongous fist on the armrest. "There was a time when you were the greatest soldier I had. Convincing Nero to burn Rome—that was a masterpiece. But now, you can barely convince a man to kill a few brats. Oh, how the mighty have fallen."

Satan clicked his fingers. A servant girl with leaches crawling all over her dirty blonde hair, brought him a tray on which stood a silver goblet filled with blood. A section of a human brain bobbed on top of the dark liquid. Satan took a swig, casting those fearsome yellow eyes back to Malik.

"If you just—" Malik began.

"SILENCE!" The King of Hell barked, his roar like thunder. He swirled his drink while pondering Malik's fate. "Mercy isn't usually my forte, but I will give you one last chance. A dead woman's remains have been disturbed and now she's in Limbo. I want you to convince her to get revenge, to kill those who killed her."

"Yes, my lord."

"The humans responsible for her demise are parents to a friend of Jared Duval. He took down two of my best warriors, so I want to make him suffer." Satan gave a carnivorous smile. "I'm allowing you to be ... creative."

"Will I eliminate him, my lord?"

"No. Unfortunately, he's protected by the ... Nazarene. Jared can be hurt but not killed. Watching his friend die will suffice for now."

"I won't let you down."

"See that you don't."

Satan nodded to one of the guards, who stepped forward, unlocking Malik's shackles that were on his dark, leathery skin. Malik sighed with relief, massaging his wrists.

"Go now, before I change my mind," Satan ordered.

Malik rose to leave, but stopped as the king continued: "Failure will see you suffer a punishment so much worse than lashings."

Malik swallowed hard before walking away.

***

When the woman opened her eyes again, she found herself standing in a long, smoky room with black walls. The place stretched out as far as her eyes could see. Victorian-style tilley lanterns hung on both sides, providing meagre light.

Where am I?

"Hello? Is anyone here?" she called out.

Only the echoing of her own words answered.

"Am I in Hell?"

Once more, only her voice, reverberating around the large room.

From some distance behind her, she suddenly heard echoey footsteps. As the figure approached, she discerned the silhouette of a tall man in what appeared to be a navy, pin-striped suit. His face was shadowed by the smoke that was around them.

"Hello?" the woman shouted.

"No need to holler, dear. I can hear you quite well. Don't fret—Malik is here. That's my name; and, from now on, I'll call you Peaches."

The mysterious stranger answered in a calm, self-assured tone as he stepped into the light. His complexion was tanned, and his ginger hair was combed to one side. She noticed a pink handkerchief, folded and sitting in the right breast pocket of his suit.

"My name isn't Peaches," she said. "It's—"

"I know what it is, but that's from a former life," Malik cut in. "I like 'Peaches'. It suits you."

It really doesn't. Wait ... Is this guy the Devil?

"Oh, no," Malik said. "That, I'm not."

Peaches frowned in embarrassment while staring at her feet.

Great, so he can read my thoughts in ... wherever we are.

"Yes, I can ... and don't worry, you'll get used to this after a while."

"Where are we?" Peaches asked.

"Isn't it obvious? We're in Limbo—a kind of halfway place between Heaven and Hell."

"Okay. Then how do I get to Heaven? Can you help me get there?"

Malik put a hand on her right arm. "I'm afraid that won't be happening anytime soon."

Peaches' face became a mask of worry. "But what can you do to help me? Are you an angel?"

"Something like that, yes. What happened to you was a travesty. An injustice. I'm here to make it right." Malik took out a long cigar from inside his jacket. "Do you mind?"

Peaches shook her head.

Malik snipped off the end with a cutter pulled from another pocket, and the cigar's tail end glowed a volcanic orange. He puffed some blue smoke before continuing: "I can take you back home and make those people pay for what they did."

"Wait, won't that stop me from getting into Heaven?"

"Darling, you're not going anywhere for a long while. Time doesn't really exist over here; but if it did, then you'd be in this place for one hundred Earth years. A long time alone, I'm sure you'll agree."

"One hundred years?" Peaches repeated, her eyes beginning to well up with tears.

"That's what I said. Of course, I could shorten that stay or make it more ... tolerable by helping you get justice."

Peaches folded her arms, raising her head and jutting her chin forward. "What's the catch?"

Malik took another drag of his cigar, exhaling more smoke. "No catch. I'm the Angel of Justice ... or in this case, vengeance. I presume you do want to make sure your murderers get what they deserve?"

They did take everything from me. They ripped me away from my baby girl. But can I really trust this guy ... angel ... whatever he is?

"The answer is yes, dear," Malik said.

Damn, I forgot he can read my mind.

"Sorry," said Peaches. "It's just … This is all so ..."

"Overwhelming? I understand; but this is a one-time offer. Do you want to spend the next hundred years here alone, or go back home and get revenge?"

"I'll never be able to speak to Anna on the phone again, or see her on the weekends," Peaches growled. "Because of *them.*"

"They did leave you to die like a dog and then hid their dirty deed afterwards. Those heartless mortals didn't give you a second thought."

He's right. I died needlessly, and they get to live. Screw them!

"Let's make them pay," she said.

Malik gave her a wide, ravenous smile, squashing the cigar with his brown leather shoe.

"Music to my ears."

He tucked one hand behind his back; and, like the gentlemen she'd read about in her mother's old Jane Austen books, he offered her the other, as if they were about to dance.

"Shall we, my dear?"

Peaches took Malik's hand. "Yes, let's. How do we go about doing this?"

"First, we'll leave here."

Malik clicked his fingers. A door of pure white light wavered to their right. She could see blue skies. Below them was Hopps Town's main street bustling with cars and people.

"I'll explain as we go through there," Malik said. "Come. Let's have some fun."

Peaches smiled as they walked hand-in-hand towards the luminous portal.

I'm coming for you both, she thought as they stepped through.

ABOUT THE AUTHOR

Aidan Lucid began writing in 2002 after having a spiritual experience. Since then, his works have appeared in national and international poetry anthologies, magazines, and e-zines. Lucid first began working on *The Zargothian Saga* trilogy while recovering from a horrific accident in 2005.

Aidan released *The Scavenger* — a horror novella — in January 2021. The first book in the *Hopps Town* series, it received many positive reviews. He followed that up with *Unlucky Charm* in January 2022 and *Dark Secrets* in 2023. In 2024, the second editions of, *The Scavenger* and *Unlucky Charm* will be released

In July 2023, Aidan won an award (Silver Literary Titan Book Award), for his book, *The Lost Son (Second Edition). A Beast Within* received the Gold Literary Titan Book Award in April 2024. He is also writing more books in The Zargpthian Saga and horror stories.

In his spare time, he likes to meditate, listen to music, and go to the movies with his wife, Claire.

THE LOST SON (SECOND EDITION)

Henry Simmons is your typical American 17-year-old kid, who likes to play games, reads comics, and ogles his dream girl, Tracey Maxwell. Henry's life takes a dramatic turn when he finds a magical golden coin. When he learns about the coin's power, the lovestruck teenager makes a wish for Tracey to be his prom date. It's granted but soon matters take a turn for the worst. On Prom Night, his date's ex beats him up. While lying on the ground, a drop of Henry's blood falls onto the coin, opening up a portal, taking him and Tracey to another world.

While there, the two teenagers meet two USAF pilots from 1945 and a talking cat named Jasper. Together they learn that they've been chosen to help King Argoth free his people from an oppressive race of creatures known as the Sadarkians. Not only must Henry learn how to properly harness the coin's power but he,

Tracey and co. must learn how to fight and prepared to do combat in an epic battle for freedom. With the Sadarkian army vastly out numbering King Argoth's though, will Henry and his little troop succeed in a world where danger lurks around every corner and nothing is at it seems.

Available on Amazon.

THE LOST SON (SECOND EDITION) AUDIOBOOK

Henry Simmons is your typical American 17-year-old kid, who likes to play games, reads comics, and ogles his dream girl, Tracey Maxwell. Henry's life takes a dramatic turn when he finds a magical golden coin. When he learns about the coin's power, the love-struck teenager makes a wish for Tracey to be his prom date. It's granted but soon matters take a turn for the worst. On Prom Night, his date's ex beats him up. While lying on the ground, a drop of Henry's blood falls onto the coin, opening up a portal, taking him and Tracey to another world.

While there, the two teenagers meet two USAF pilots from 1945 and a talking cat named Jasper. Together they learn that they've been chosen to help King Argoth free his people from an oppressive race of creatures known as the Sadarkians. Not only must Henry learn how to properly harness the coin's power but he, Tracey and co. must learn how to fight and prepared to do combat in an epic battle for freedom. With the Sadarkian army vastly out numbering King Argoth's though, will Henry and his little troop succeed in a world where danger lurks around every corner and nothing is at it seems.

Available on Audible.

DEADLY PURSUITS

A New Evil and Army Rises Against Zargothia

When Henry defeated the Sadarkians, he thought the worst was over. He was wrong. Slyvanon, the twisted advisor to the former Sadarkian king, has awakened Jadin – an unrelenting assassin – with a single mission: to eliminate Henry.

Jadin crosses over into Henry's world, hunting him with precision, heedless of who might be caught in the crossfire. With his best friend Joey and Tracey, the girl who's always just out of his reach, Henry is swept into a terrifying chase that hurls them back into Zargothia — where hell seems to be gradually breaking loose.

As Henry takes on his role as the protector, he stumbles upon newfound power. But he will need every ounce of it to face what lies ahead.

Slyvanon's dark schemes are far from over, and a new army is rising.

THE SCAVENGER AUDIOBOOK

Three separate wishes. One twisted nightmare!

Just like Hopps Town, their humble home, Jessica Barlow, Jared Duval, and Adrian Cole are fostering dark secrets. Plagued by loss, cruelty, and physical abuse, these friends are kindred spirits, bound by anguish and elusive dreams. They're soon to find the key to change, but any happy future will demand they face a haunting past and brave a lethal present.

Deep in the forest on the outskirts of town, aging and nearly forgotten, there stands a well from another time. Happening upon this relic, Adrian goads his companions to join him in making a wish. Soon, difficult though it is to admit, their luckless lives do seem to shift. The only problem is, the changes aren't at all as they'd imagined. Seemingly, they've only left the pan to face the fire.

Should they hope to both survive and thrive, they'll need to pool their wits and draw on mystic inner-power. Solving Hopps Town's greatest mystery now means life or death.

Available on Audible.

A BEAST WITHIN

Have you experienced true terror? For three criminals, they're about to face it head-on!

Fresh out of prison, Jeremy vows to steer clear of a life of crime and clean up his act. But he quickly realizes that to the world, he will always be an ex-con and plunges back into his old ways. The perfect opportunity presents itself in the form of his best friend, Stephen, and his spunky girlfriend, Natalie.

After a failed bank robbery, Jeremy and his accomplices' identities are made. So, they find refuge in the home of a typical Christian family. Their getaway should have been smooth sailing…after all it was three armed criminals against the wholesome Boyd family.

But the Boyds are hiding dark secrets of their own...

Also available as an audiobook on Audible.

"I loved this story. From the first page I was hooked! There are twists and turns."

- Hanna (Booksirens reviewer).

***A Beast Within* received the Gold Literary Titan Book Award in April 2024.**

DID YOU ENJOY THE BOOK?

So, what did you think of, *Unlucky Charm (Second Edition)*? Did you like/dislike it? I'd love to hear your thoughts by you posting a review. Each one helps get a book noticed; but it also tells an author what he or she is doing right or wrong, so they can improve their future books. At the end of the day, we authors want to please you guys, the readers. So, please leave a review.

Thank you.

JOIN MY MAILING LIST

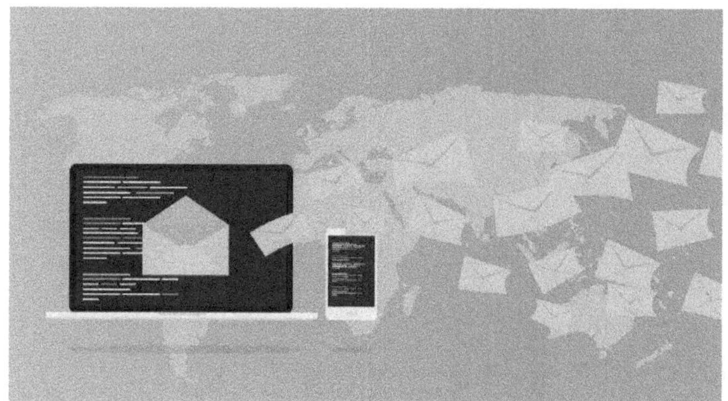

Be sure to sign up to my mailing list today to be notified of the following:

- Upcoming releases
- Free ebook offers
- E-book discounts and special price promotions
- Competitions
- New merchandise

Visit this link to subscribe: https://www.subscribepage.com/hopps_town_mailinglist

CONNECT WITH AIDAN ON:

https://www.instagram.com/aidanlucidauthor/

www.ingramcontent.com/pod-product-compliance
Lightning Source LLC
LaVergne TN
LVHW050557160826
845677LV00011B/2352

* 9 7 9 8 2 3 0 1 9 0 8 2 0 *